THE
THRIFTY GUIDE TO
MEDIEVAL TIMES

A HANDBOOK FOR TIME TRAVELERS

THE
THRIFTY GUIDE TO
MEDIEVAL TIMES

A HANDBOOK FOR TIME TRAVELERS

Jonathan W. Stokes
illustrated by Xavier Bonet

PUFFIN

PUFFIN
An imprint of Penguin Random House LLC, New York

First published in the United States of America by Puffin Books,
an imprint of Penguin Random House LLC, 2019

Visit us online at penguinrandomhouse.com

LIBRARY OF CONGRESS CATALOGING-IN-PUBLICATION DATA IS AVAILABLE.
ISBN 9780451480286

Printed in United States of America
Book design, maps, and graphs by Mariam Quraishi

PREFACE

The Thrifty Guide to Medieval Times: A Handbook for Time Travelers was published holographically by Time Corp in the year 2164. It offers a complete vacation package for tourists visiting the Middle Ages. A careless time traveler accidentally lost a copy of this handy guidebook in our own era, along with guides to ancient Rome, ancient Greece, and the American Revolution. A New York publishing house decided to republish these books, beating Time Corp to market by more than a century.

The Thrifty Guide to Medieval Times provides useful information for the practical time traveler:

- How can I avoid being attacked by rampaging Mongols?

- How can I avoid being attacked by pillaging Huns?

- What are my health-care options if I catch the bubonic plague?

- And most importantly, why on earth would anyone want to travel to the Middle Ages?

This guide answers your hunger for knowledge with an all-you-can-eat buffet of information. There is helpful advice on how to avoid being bled to death by a medieval doctor, how to survive a witch trial, and how to keep a Viking raid from ruining your lunch plans. So stop brushing your teeth and throw away your shampoo bottle. What follows is the original *Thrifty Guide to Medieval Times*, as it was discovered on a sidewalk outside Frank's Pizza in Manhattan in 2019. . . .

THE THRIFTY GUIDE TO MEDIEVAL TIMES
A HANDBOOK FOR TIME TRAVELERS

TIME CORP!™ THE FUTURE IS NOW!
BUT ALSO TOMORROW. AND YESTERDAY.™

TIME CORP!™ SERVING YESTERDAY, FOR A BETTER TOMORROW, TODAY.™

INTRODUCTION BY TIME CORP CEO AND CORPORATE OVERLORD,
FINN GREENQUILL

Congratulations on purchasing *The Thrifty Guide to Medieval Times: A Handbook for Time Travelers*, the best book ever published, except for all the other Thrifty Guides.

A lot of people ask me, "Finn, what are Medieval Times, and how can I spend lots of money on them?" In a nutshell, Medieval Times—also known as the Middle Ages—are a long period in European history when it was extremely difficult to find a decent plumber. After the fall of the Western Roman Empire in AD 476, Europe was ravaged by attacking Goths, Vandals, Huns, and furious time travelers who had just found out their tickets to the Middle Ages were nonrefundable. For the next thousand years, "Europe" and "civilization" were two words you might not rush to use in the same sentence. Hardly anyone in Europe could read or write, and even bathing fell out of fashion. Historians used to refer to this dangerous time as "the Dark Ages," which sounds very rock-and-roll. But I, Finn Greenquill, am in the business of selling vacation packages. So—taking a page from modern historians and our publicity department—we now refer to these turbulent times as "the Middle Ages," and the more dangerous parts as "thrilling." Some time travelers may be interested in visiting the Americas, Africa, or Asia during this time period. Those vacations will be coming up in future Time Corp travel packages, but they'll cost more because they are generally more pleasant. If there is anything else you would like to spend your money on, may I suggest buying a copy of *The Thrifty Guide to Spending Lots of Money*, which retails for $999,999? Enjoy your trip!

Your trustworthy friend,

Finn Greenquill

Finn Greenquill
CEO and Corporate Overlord, Time Corp

TIME CORP LIMITATION OF LIABILITY

By reading this time travel guide, you agree to and accept the following:

1. Finn Greenquill may, with no advance notice, show up at your house for dinner.

2. If you discover a lost historical artifact, you will return it to Finn Greenquill rather than the person it actually belongs to.

3. Twice a day you will stick your head out a window and shout Finn Greenquill's name as loud as you can.

4. If you go back in time and accidentally obliterate your great-grandparents, erasing yourself from existence, Finn Greenquill gets to keep all your stuff.

5. If you are kidnapped by Vikings, Finn Greenquill reserves the right to resell your copy of this book.

6. Finn Greenquill is not to be held responsible for anything, ever.

7. If you can find a way to prevent disco from happening, Finn Greenquill will automatically make you vice president of Time Corp.

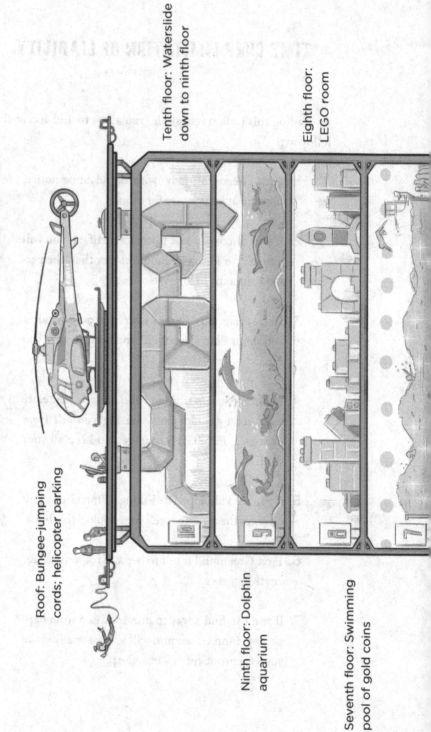

FINN GREENQUILL'S
HIGH-RISE LUXURY APARTMENT

Roof: Bungee-jumping cords; helicopter parking

Tenth floor: Waterslide down to ninth floor

Ninth floor: Dolphin aquarium

Eighth floor: LEGO room

Seventh floor: Swimming pool of gold coins

Sixth floor: 3-D
movie theater

Fourth floor:
Chocolate living
room

First floor: Parking
garage for limousine
and also for cheetah-
drawn golden chariot

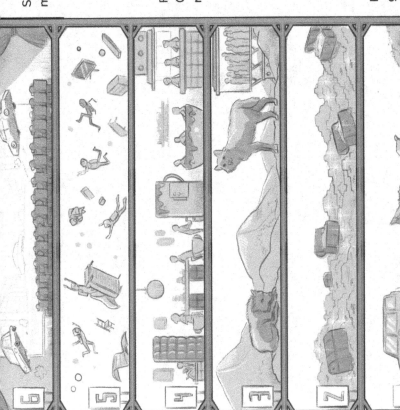

Fifth floor: Zero-gravity bedroom, for comfortable sleep

Third floor: Dire
wolf pen

Second floor: Precious
jewels collection

CONTENTS

INTRODUCTION
THE BASICS OF TIME TRAVEL

Who was Genghis Khan? What made him tick? Was he more of a dog person or a cat person? Why did he slaughter 11 percent of the world's population?

The problem with asking questions of major historical figures is that most of them are too dead to answer.

Enter time travel. Sure, it's so expensive, it may take you three centuries to save up for a trip, but that's exactly why we have time machines. On the following pages, we'll teach you all you need to know—or at least the bare minimum—to time travel.

Your Time Machine

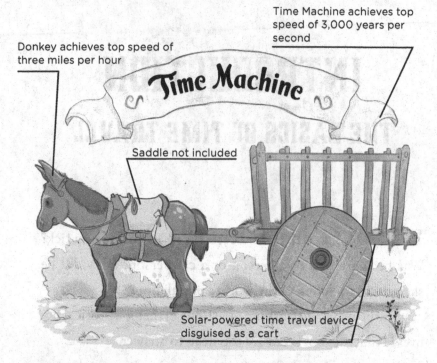

Donkey achieves top speed of three miles per hour

Time Machine achieves top speed of 3,000 years per second

Saddle not included

Solar-powered time travel device disguised as a cart

1. The Time Corp Time Machine Donkey Cart™

Okay, we know what you're thinking: *a donkey cart?* I paid three hundred years of savings for this time travel vacation, and all you're giving me is *a donkey cart?*

The short answer is: yes. Here at Time Corp, we care about safety first. If we sent you into the Middle Ages with anything fancier than a wooden cart pulled by a half-starved donkey, you'd probably be robbed within nanoseconds of your arrival. Riding around on a donkey cart, you will quickly win the admiration of the locals, most of whom are so poor, they can barely afford to ride around on their own two feet.

Your donkey is genetically enhanced for your comfort, with all-natural leather seating: namely, its back. The cart contains your Time Corp solar-powered time travel device.* All other amenities cost extra. Enjoy your ride!

2. Time Corp Costume Department

Fashion is everything. Time Corp can't have you showing up to William the Conqueror's coronation in 1066 wearing your space pants and bionic arms. Your clothes will be so out of fashion, you will either die of embarrassment, or die when William the Conqueror's bodyguards kill you for being a foreign spy.

The key to safe time traveling is blending in. Often, the best way to do this is by posing as a common villager. You'll want an ensemble that says, *I'm here! I'm illiterate! And I have an average life expectancy of thirty years!*

For a modest fee, the Time Corp costume department will dress you in the cheapest, dirtiest, most flea-bitten rags we can find. We'll even rub your clothes in manure free of charge, to give them that distinctive tenth-century aroma.

---

* Even though this period was once called "the Dark Ages," your solar-powered time machine will still work.

3. Time Corp Laboratories

Here at Time Corp Labs, moderately paid Time Corp scientists are constantly testing new gadgets to help you enjoy your vacation in style and comfort. Below is a taste of some of the exciting products we will be introducing, just as soon as our legal department can settle all of our outstanding claims.

Wolf Whistle™—Surrounded by angry villagers? They've seen your advanced technology and think you're a witch? Need to make a hasty exit? Just blow Time Corp's handy new Wolf Whistle™ and you will summon every wolf within a ten-mile radius. That will send the villagers packing and give them something else to think about besides witches.*

Nuclear-Powered Jousting Kit—Challenged to a duel by a medieval knight? Never fear! The Nuclear-Powered Jousting

* **WARNING:** Time Corp has not yet invented Wolf Repellent.

Kit is here! Impress your friends and never lose a jousting match with this ultrasonic lance.*

Viking Repellent—Now in a handy spray can. Just spritz yourself before visiting the Viking-infested waters of the North Sea. Remember to spray it evenly and don't forget behind your ears. In emergencies, you can simply spray the repellent directly on the Vikings themselves.†

* **WARNING:** The lance has a six-kiloton discharge and a three-mile blast radius. Be sure you have radioactive shield armor and a Time Corp life insurance policy.

† **WARNING:** Viking Repellent is highly attractive to both sharks and bears.

1

GOTHS, HUNS, VANDALS, AND OTHER PEOPLE YOU WOULDN'T WANT OVER FOR DINNER

THINGS YOU WILL NEED

1. A medieval cloak, to blend in
2. A horse, to escape Huns
3. A dagger, for protection
4. Life insurance

THE EARLY MIDDLE AGES, EUROPE 490

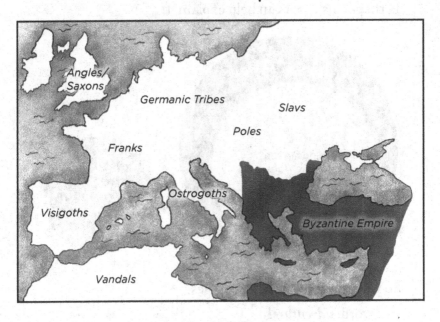

Welcome to the Middle Ages!

If you've chosen our Middle Ages time travel vacation, you either have very little money to spend or absolutely no regard for your own personal safety. After the fall of the Western Roman Empire in AD 476,* western Europe fractures into warring tribes, and western civilization takes a few ginormous steps backward. For the next thousand years, Europe is wracked by invasions, famines, plagues, poverty, pirates, and deeply questionable fashion choices. The reason the Middle Ages is our most affordable travel package is that your chance of survival is

---

* The Roman Empire ruled much of Europe for centuries and provided a lot of the perks of civilization: theater, bridges, poetry, sewers, law, art, and a touch of class. For more on the Romans, do yourself a favor and read one of the greatest books in history: *The Thrifty Guide to Ancient Rome: A Handbook for Time Travelers*.

even smaller than a holiday bonus from Finn Greenquill.

Perhaps this chart can help explain it:

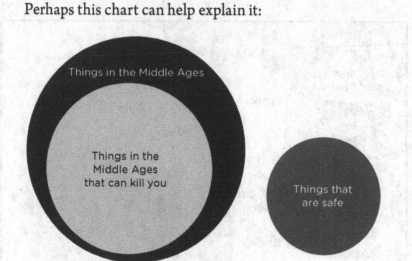

So why travel to the Middle Ages?

In a word: *adventure!*

Well, that's what Time Corp's marketing department came up with. The truth is, much of the groundwork for modern society is laid during the Middle Ages. Our language, our laws, our countries, our food, even our method of writing music—so much of who we are today is created during this tumultuous time period.

The Middle Ages is such a giant chunk of time, historians have carved it into three bite-size pieces: the Early Middle Ages (AD 476–1000), High Middle Ages (AD 1000–1300), and Late Middle Ages (AD 1300–1500). The bad news is, you are now in the Early Middle Ages. The Roman Empire is crumbling, and bloodthirsty barbarian invaders are closing in from all directions....

Enjoy your vacation!

A MESSAGE FROM THE TIME TRAVEL CUSTOMS BUREAU

WARNING! The following items may not be transported into the Middle Ages:

- A toothbrush
- A bottle of shampoo
- Pretty much any medicine
- Pretty much most technology
- Foods Europe hasn't discovered yet, like chocolate, vanilla, tomatoes, corn, potatoes, avocados, blueberries, peanuts, and bananas. Oh, also turkeys. No matter how tempting it is, please do not bring turkeys to the Middle Ages.

Western Civilization Was Fun While It Lasted

For centuries, the Roman Empire has been the center of stability and civilization in Europe. The Romans have created world-class art, architecture, and scientific advances. They've built thousands of miles of roads to connect the far-flung corners of their empire. They've built aqueducts for clean drinking water. They have lawyers and courts of law.

But this party is about to get crashed in a major way....

Meet the Goths

The first group to ravage Rome is the Goths. They are warriors from Scandinavia* who sweep through the European continent, breaking pretty much everything. In a few hundred years the Norwegians and Danes will invent fast ships and become Viking raiders. But for now, think of the Goths as just Vikings without boats. So the north is a source of centuries of trouble for western Europeans.

When the Goths look at Rome, they don't see a glorious symbol of human achievement; they see dollar signs.† Rome is crammed full of unfathomable wealth: gold, silver, jewels, ivory, coins, and priceless art. The Goths plunder Rome, stealing everything that isn't tied down. Alaric I is the Goth leader who has the pleasure of sacking Rome in AD 410, and the great displeasure of dying immediately afterward when he catches fever in a storm.

Theodoric the Great is the Goth leader who kills Odoacer, the king of Italy, at a dinner party on March 15, AD 493. Theodoric and Odoacer have just signed a peace treaty and are celebrating. The thing is, Theodoric isn't big on peace treaties. He wants Italy for himself. He chooses this moment to draw his sword and stab the king in the neck. King Odoacer's last words are, "Where is

---

* Or possibly Poland. Historians honestly aren't sure. If you meet some Goths, ask them!

† The Goths are also looking for a new homeland, and Italy seems like a great place to settle down.

God?" Theodoric then has Odoacer's wife stoned to death. The lesson is, if Theodoric invites you to any dinner parties, it's best to just make up an excuse and stay home. Suffice it to say, the Goths quickly take over Italy.

The Visigoths, Ostrogoths, Burgundians, and Vandals are all tribes from Scandinavia and northern Europe. It doesn't take them long to take over a large part of Europe and North Africa.

Helpful Hints:
Blending In

If you want to fly under the radar on your medieval time travel vacation, it may be safest to pose as a villager. If you dress as a soldier, you're liable to get attacked by a rampaging Goth, which will put a dent in either you or your afternoon plans.

A village is often no more than fifty to one hundred people. Most villagers live their entire lives within a twenty-mile radius and rarely meet people with different languages or nationalities. Historians estimate the average medieval villager meets fewer than two hundred people in their entire lifetime. Books are incredibly expensive because they are handwritten. Most people have never even seen a book, let alone know how to read. Don't say anything too smart and you should blend in just fine.

MALE VILLAGER

FEMALE VILLAGER

Teeth don't rot because there is almost no sugar in the medieval diet. However, bread is gritty from the millstones used to grind grain, and this wears down everyone's teeth.

Soap exists, but shampoo doesn't. One of the ways a woman will court a man is by combing the lice out of his hair. It's very romantic.

Men often wear a tunic, wool stockings, breeches, and a cloak.

Women wear a long wool skirt called a kirtle, an apron, wool stockings, and a cloak.

EMPIRE OF ATTILA THE HUN, 453

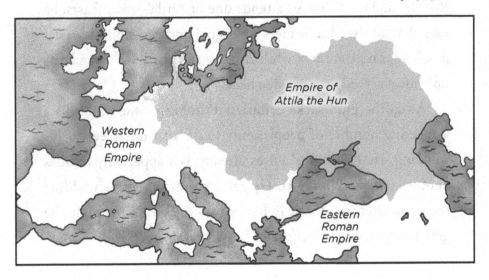

Attila the Hun

The Burgundians, Vandals, and Goths aren't the only ones busy spoiling the Romans' party. The Huns are a tribe of warrior horsemen from central Asia who attack the Roman Empire from the east and scare everyone witless. Hun fighters are equally skilled with the bow and the lance and can fight from horseback. Even the Goths are afraid of them: the Goths begin attacking the Roman Empire partly just to get away from the Huns.

By AD 440, a terrifying warlord named Attila the Hun has left Russia, crossed the Danube River, and begun looting and pillaging his merry way across Europe. He is not picky about whom he kills: he slaughters Goths, Vandals, Burgundians, and Romans alike. To buy loyalty, Attila gives all his plunder to his generals and supporters. He himself remains poor.* When the

....

* Finn Greenquill does not agree with this policy.

Roman diplomat Priscus attends one of Attila's great feasts, he sees that all the Hun leaders wear gold and gemstones and eat fine foods on silver trays, while Attila wears plain clothes and eats only meat served on a wooden plate.

Attila the Hun sacks countless European cities and kills a staggering number of people, only to die of a nosebleed at his wedding. He has several wives already, but apparently decides another one couldn't hurt. He gets very drunk at his wedding feast and later passes out in his bedroom. During the night, he gets a nosebleed that suffocates him in his sleep.

The Fall of the Roman Empire

The destruction of Rome is good news for looting Goths and Huns, but bad news for western civilization. The secrets to creating magnificent buildings, bridges, and aqueducts die with the Romans. The new invaders have no idea how to bake bricks or mix cement, so beautiful Roman roadways, houses, towns, and cities gradually fall into ruin.

With cities destroyed, most people become farmers or laborers. There are few jobs that require people to learn how to read. Within a couple of generations, hardly anyone in Europe can decipher Roman or Greek texts. For the next thousand years, the knowledge of the ancients is mostly lost. If you are traveling to this time period, remember to pack a novel or two—you won't find many good books lying around in the Early Middle Ages.

Helpful Hints:
your early medieval hovel

Considering the mobs of foreigners galloping into Europe, there are surprisingly few decent hotels. Good luck staying with the Huns; they're nomads. It's hard to find a hotel when it picks up and moves every night.

Your best bet is to live in a villager's hovel. Most villagers live in these one- or two-room huts. Everyone sleeps crammed together on the floor and it's very smoky because fireplaces and brick chimneys aren't invented until the 1200s. You may also notice a bit of an odor because the family animals—like a pig, goat, or cow—often live inside the home.

Don't worry too much about the animals. Medieval farm animals are actually tiny because of malnourishment and lack of breeding. A full-grown bull is around the size of a modern calf. Sheep are only one-third the size they are today. So don't feel like you are sleeping in a barn; picture it more like you are sleeping with a bunch of snacks.

Helpful Hints:
What to eat in the Early Middle Ages

The one thing you won't have to worry about in the Early Middle Ages is putting on weight. Villagers often eat a horrible concoction called pottage. Pottage is basically anything the villagers dug up in the field that day, boiled in a pot until it's mush. Of all the horrors of the Middle Ages, pottage may take the crown.

Bread can be even more dangerous. When villagers run out of wheat, they use old rye to bake their bread. Aged rye often contains a fungus that causes villagers to hallucinate, lose their limbs to gangrene, or even die.

If you're hanging out in a village, on very special occasions, you may get to eat more expensive foods like meat, cheese, or eggs. But the rest of the time, get used to bread and pottage and just be glad you're not being hunted down by Huns.*

* If you're jonesing for some fancier food, you'll have to wait until the High Middle Ages, when we sample a royal feast on page 91.

The Moors

Also laying waste to the former Roman Empire are the Moors, a fierce gaggle of Muslim tribes sailing in from North Africa. Beginning in AD 711, the Moors make a pretty decent go of invading southern Europe, conquering Spain, Corsica, and eventually parts of Italy. They practice a religion called Islam that originates in the Arabian Peninsula in the early seventh century and quickly spreads across three continents.

Being conquered by the Moors isn't all bad news. Unlike the illiterate Goths and Huns, the Muslim invaders value science, literature, art, and medicine. They introduce Europe to the Hindu-Arabic number system, the system we still use. It's way less clunky than Roman numerals and contains one nifty innovation—the zero. Have you tried doing multiplication with just Roman numerals? It's enough to make you want to destroy the Roman Empire a second time.

The Moors bring many other ideas to Europe. You may have them to thank for algebra and chemistry, both of which names are derived from Arabic words.* The Moors are also responsible for teaching the Europeans new ideas about astronomy, agriculture, and medicine. They even bring Europe an Indian strategy game called chess.

....

* The Moors didn't invent algebra or chemistry, but it was Muslim thinkers who made most of the useful contributions to these subjects in the Middle Ages.

HeLpfuL HiNts:
SCHOOL

In the Early Middle Ages, you may have to run from in-vading barbarians, you may have to sleep in a hut with a donkey, but you won't have to go to school. There's really no point in learning to read when there are hardly any books.

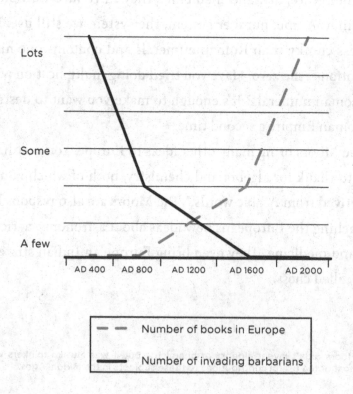

Lots

Some

A few

AD 400   AD 800   AD 1200   AD 1600   AD 2000

- - - Number of books in Europe

—— Number of invading barbarians

If you have a hankering for some schooling, you really only have two choices: be born rich or become a monk. If you are a rich nobleman's son, you may be able to afford a private tutor. Or, if you go live in a monastery, you will have access to some of the only books in Europe. If you stick around in the Middle Ages for a few centuries, Oxford University will be founded in England around 1096. It still exists today. Other universities begin sprouting up around that time to help train priests.

HeLpfuL HiNts:
seeiNg a ðoctoR

It's funny they call this the Middle Ages, since almost no one actually reaches middle age. Between 30 and 50 percent of people in this time period do not even survive childhood.*

If you get sick or are injured by a homicidal Hun, whatever you do, for the love of all that is sacred, DO NOT SEE A MEDIEVAL DOCTOR. Medicine is not quite up to snuff yet, and a trip to a doctor can often result in death.

---

* People in the Middle Ages have a real knack for dying in childbirth or being struck down by disease. The average life expectancy is about thirty years. People who are lucky enough to survive past age thirty, however, do stand a decent chance of reaching their middle ages in the Middle Ages.

In the Middle Ages, surgery is practiced by barbers. That's right: the person who cuts your hair is the same person who cuts off your frostbitten leg. The familiar red and white stripes of the barber pole originally come from the red and white strips of bloody bandages.

With little science, few schools, and fewer books, most early medieval medicine is superstition and guesswork. Feeling sick? You might have too much blood. A medieval barber can fix that by covering you in bloodsucking leeches.

Have a headache? You might have too much pressure in your head. For a small price, a medieval barber will happily drill a hole in your head for you. There. How does your headache feel now?

One popular healing cure is to go on a long pilgrimage to a religious site, preferably one that has a relic, like a bone or body part of a dead saint. Under the weather? Want to curl up in bed? Never mind that. Just walk to a cathedral in Spain!

DOCTORS IN MEDIEVAL EUROPE

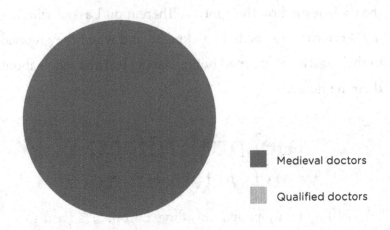

Medieval doctors

Qualified doctors

European medicine lags behind medicine in the Middle East. Here is an actual account from a Syrian doctor* who had the misfortune of working alongside a medieval European doctor:

The Europeans brought me a knight with an abscess in his leg. . . . I applied a poultice until the abscess opened and became well. . . . Then a European doctor came and said, "This man knows nothing about treatment." The doctor said to the knight, "Which wouldst thou prefer, living with one leg or dying with two?" The knight replied, "Living with one leg." The doctor said, "Bring me a strong knight and a sharp ax." A knight came with an ax. The doctor laid the patient's leg on a

....

* This account was written down by Usamah Ibn Munqidh, a Muslim warrior, in 1188. For a map of the Middle East, see page 53.

block of wood and bade the knight to chop it off. The knight struck but the leg was not severed. He dealt another blow and the patient died on the spot.... Thereupon I asked whether my services were needed any longer, and when they replied in the negative I returned home, having learned much about their medicine.

HeLpfuL HiNts:
WHO IS attacking you?

With so many people invading Europe, it's hard to keep track of them all. Here is a quick guide to help you figure out who is currently attacking you.

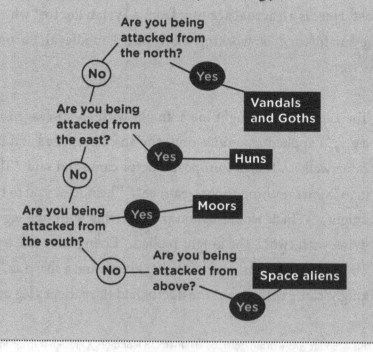

HeLpfuL HinTs:
ReLiGions in THe miDDLe ages

Religion is a huge part of people's lives in the Middle Ages, and a huge part of their deaths, too. Many of the wars in this time period are fought over religion. On the bright side, many of the great artistic achievements of the age are inspired by religion, too. Here's a quick guide to the major religions you'll encounter.

Celtic Pagans "There are at least two hundred gods, and they live in nature all around us!"

Viking Pagans "There are twelve gods, and they live in Asgard!"

Roman Pagans "There are twelve gods, and they live on Mount Olympus!"

Jews "There is only one god!"

Christians "There is only one god, and his son is Jesus Christ!"

Muslims "There is only one god, and his prophet is Muhammad!"

Charlemagne

Goths, Vandals, Huns, Moors . . . you get the picture. Outside invaders beat up western Europe from all sides. It's not until AD 768 that Europe finally gets its own homegrown warlord to beat itself up. Charlemagne* is a Frankish† king with a bee in his bonnet to conquer Europe and turn everyone into Christians.

Christianity has become the religion of the Roman Empire that once ruled much of western and southern Europe. But Europe is a pretty big continent and much of it is still chock-full of pagans—people who worship many gods. Meanwhile Spain and southern Italy are ruled by the Moors, who are Muslims.

Charlemagne finds his mission in life: make war on everyone to teach them to be peace-loving Christians. He fights Muslim

....

* His name translates to "Charles the Great" or, as we at Time Corp like to call him, "Big Charlie."

† As a Frank, Charlemagne spoke German but lived in France. Go figure.

Moors and pagan Europeans and even massacres 4,500 pagan tribesmen in Germany. That'll teach them to love peace. The pope—the most prominent leader of Christianity in Europe—thinks Charlemagne is simply *the best*. After all, Charlemagne is great at boosting church attendance.* Every battle he wages is like a membership drive. For all his fighting, Charlemagne is slowly succeeding in uniting western Europe under one government and one religion. A lot of Europeans who don't have time machines think this will result in an era of great peace. . . .

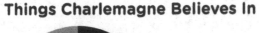

Things Charlemagne Believes In

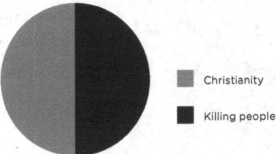

Christianity

Killing people

Things Christians Are Supposed to Believe In

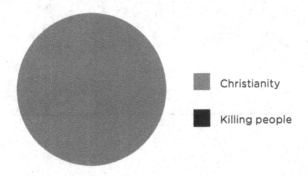

Christianity

Killing people

....

* Not only that, but Charlemagne saved Pope Leo III from being blinded and having his tongue cut out after he was accused of lying in court. Also, to top it off, Charlemagne's father gave central Italy to the pope as a gift.

There's just one problem. Charlemagne's empire is so big, it's now bumping up against its violent Scandinavian neighbors to the north. Scandinavia is the land that produced the Goths and the Vandals. And this land is about to produce an even deadlier band of raiders: the Vikings.

CHARLEMAGNE'S EMPIRE, 814

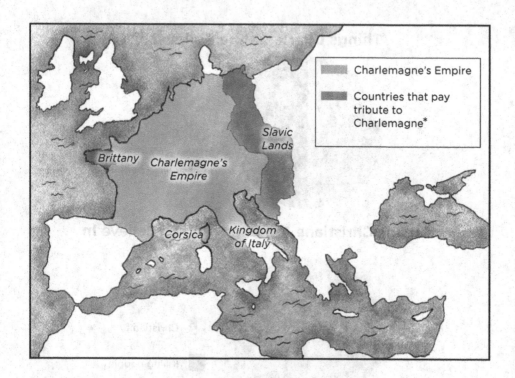

* "Paying tribute" means these countries pay Charlemagne to not attack them. It's a nifty way for Charlemagne to pocket some extra money.

According to one story, toward the end of Charlemagne's life, he is eating breakfast on the French coast when he spots Viking warships on the horizon. The ships are so fast, they vanish by the time Charlemagne's troops draw their swords and reach the shore. Charlemagne bursts into tears. His servants ask why he is crying. Charlemagne tells them it is because he knows there is nothing he can do to stop the Vikings. . . .

2

THE VIKING RAIDERS

THINGS YOU WILL NEED

1. A fashionable helmet*

2. A mace or iron cudgel

3. A war hammer

4. A sweet beard

5. A battle-ax

6. Bug spray

7. A cloak made of reindeer hide

8. Dramamine if you get seasick

....

* Horns are optional. People often picture Vikings wearing helmets with horns on them, but the Vikings don't actually do this. The sad part about time traveling is learning which famous parts of history are just rumors.

If you have some pillaging to do, there is really no better way to scratch that itch than to go on a Viking raid. And the best thing about the past? It's extremely affordable. In the future, one hundred pounds of gold will not even buy you fifty pounds of gold. But in AD 800, one hundred pounds of gold will buy you a whole fleet of brand-spanking-new Viking longships and an enthusiastic raiding party. So grow your beard, grab your war hammer, and bludgeon a villager, because it's time to visit the age of the Vikings!

Viking 101

For centuries, the Scandinavians have been in the business of raiding Europe, and business is good. But when Scandinavians go raiding, they tend to do it on foot.* Their ships are slow and they can't travel out of sight from land for risk of being capsized.

This all changes around the 700s. Scandinavians invent a new ship hull that won't capsize in tall waves. Now the Vikings can cross oceans. But that's not all! The larger hulls can also support masts with sails that double the speed of the ships.

Now the Vikings command the fastest ships in the world and they don't even need to blister their hands rowing. The speed of a Viking longship is incredible. It averages five to ten knots (roughly six to eleven miles) per hour, and with a perfect wind, it can hit

---

* The word "Viking" means raiding. This is where the Vikings get their name.

fifteen knots. So a Viking ship can easily cover forty miles in an average day. This far outpaces foot soldiers or even horsemen. Vikings can now raid a village and vanish long before an opposing army can arrive.

Bottom line: Europe is in for a rough couple of centuries.

Helpful Hints:
your viking Longship

Your longship is powered by wind, Vikings, and, failing that, slaves. If you use oar slaves to power your ship, they may be English, Irish, Finnish, or whoever you happen to have handy.* The Vikings do a brisk trade in capturing and selling people all over Europe.

A drummer at the rear of the ship may pound a beat on a rawhide drum while the oarsmen, chained two per oar, row you wherever you need to go. You will navigate by the sun, the stars, or releasing birds to see if they find land. There is only one deck on the ship, so everyone just sleeps on their benches, even if it is raining or snowing. This is a charming and efficient way to travel, all the way up until your slaves pass out or die from exhaustion.†

* Our modern word "slave" is actually named after the Slavs—a group of Eastern European people with an unfortunate aptitude for getting themselves sold into slavery, first by the Romans and later by Germans and Vikings.

† Time Corp offers roadside assistance for a very reasonable fee of seven hundred silver pieces.

Your Viking Hall

If you visit the home of a Viking chieftain, you might expect to find a giant castle. But in this time period, even the most successful Viking leader just lives in a simple one-story hall. The room's dirt floor is covered with straw, which is often strewn with garbage and crawling with vermin. When the straw gets too filthy, the Vikings simply throw fresh straw on top.

There's a fire to keep you somewhat warm. It's essentially a bonfire—there is no chimney—so there's a constant risk your Viking hall will burn down. Someday, once Europeans finally figure out how the ancient Romans made bricks, chimneys will begin to appear. Only then will houses become stable enough to support a second story.

A Viking hall is one long room. The whole idea of having a bunch of separate rooms takes a long time to evolve because windows and doors are really expensive. The word "bedroom" doesn't appear until Shakespeare's time, in the 1500s.

Ragnar's Viking Hall

Parking: Warship dock
Noise Level: Terrified screams
Décor: ★★★★
Wheelchair Accessible: No ✕
Service: ★
War-Horse Accessible: Yes
Cost: $
Accepts Credit Cards: No ✕
Happy Hour: Never ✕✕
Accepts Tributes: Yes
Attire: Smart casual
Accepts Ransoms: Yes

There is a reason you don't find a lot of Viking restaurants in the future. Viking food is bland, to put it mildly. Finn Greenquill thinks it's possible the Vikings started raiding Europe just to find a decent club sandwich. Nevertheless, here is a place you can eat while visiting the Viking age.

Ragnar is a war chief who will invite you into his hall in exchange for a few good stories and a few good gold pieces. His food is a refreshing fusion of somewhat edible and barely edible cuisine.* The vegetarian options are . . . limited. You can order whatever you like as long as it's mutton. Mutton is lightly flavored with a variety of spices, including mead, cabbage, sweat, horse, and more mutton.

Ragnar's is a typical Viking hall. Blood-chilling tales of the Viking war gods in Valhalla† are told by the roaring fire. The festivities usually end with much song, merriment, and someone getting stabbed. Don't expect much in the way of service. Instead of napkins, you can literally wipe your hands on a dog. Seriously. Swedish Vallhunds are trained to circle the table like walking napkins, allowing guests to wipe off their mutton-greased hands.

Sound like fun? Then grab a mutton chop, wipe your hands on a dog, and head on down to Ragnar's Viking Hall!

Here is what some of our readers say about Ragnar's Viking Hall:

★★ "The spiced mutton was tenderized by a club. I was tenderized by a club, too."   —Mike S., Raleigh, NC

★ "When I complained about the rude service, my waiter burned down an entire village."   —Sam B., Pasadena, CA

★ "I would have given this restaurant four stars, but my leg got shattered by a war hammer."   —Phil N., Brooklyn, NY

....

* Ragnar does not care about your food allergies. You will find him very insensitive about your gluten sensitivity and very intolerant of your lactose intolerance.

† Valhalla is a Viking heaven. It's a mead hall where drunken war heroes exchange battle stories for all eternity.

HeLpfuL HiNts:
tippiNG BY time period

Nothing is more awkward than tipping the wrong amount.
Here is a helpful guide to tipping throughout the ages.*

Year	Average Service	Good Service	Great Service
9000 BC	Spare waiter's life	One pebble	A bear tooth
100 BC	One face smack	One copper coin	Two face smacks
AD 500	A lump of coal	Two copper coins	One child
AD 1999	18%	20%	22%
AD 2019	20%	22%	A great online review
AD 2030	25%	An epic poem	30%
AD 2061	90%	A unicorn's mane	A uranium mine
AD 3231	An island	Seven comets	A small moon

* Source: Finn Greenquill's personal opinions

VIKINGS GO VIRAL!

Lands Raided, Conquered, or Settled by Vikings, 700-1100

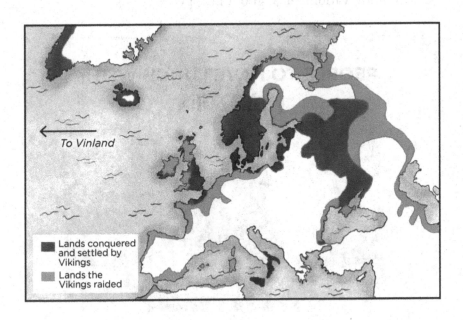

To Vinland

Lands conquered and settled by Vikings

Lands the Vikings raided

The Viking Conquest

For the next few centuries, the Vikings are unstoppable. Vikings sack major European cities from London to Paris, from Kiev to Cologne. They explore the North Atlantic, creating settlements in Iceland and Greenland. A Viking named Leif Erikson is the first European to set foot in North America: he starts a settlement in Canada five hundred years before the time of Columbus. Vikings conquer much of Ireland and found the capital city of

Dublin. They start the Russian royal family and create the kingdom of Russia. They forge trade routes that stretch from England to Baghdad. And along the way, they spread many new ideas and cultural innovations throughout Europe.

PEOPLE TO HAVE LUNCH WITH:
HASTEIN

Hastein is a famous Viking who really gets around. He raids and pillages France, England, Spain, Italy, and North Africa.

For a good time, join Hastein on his most daring raid. Set your time machine for the city of Luna, Italy, in AD 859. Hastein's ships are sighted by the town guards, who ring alarm bells and lock the city gates. With no way to assault the now fortified city, Hastein turns to his famous Viking cunning. He waves a flag of truce, claims to be sick, and tells the city guards he wants to convert to Christianity before he dies. The Christians are suspicious, but allow Hastein into the city under heavy guard. Hastein, appearing to be deathly ill, is carried into the town church on a stretcher and baptized by the town bishop, with the local count acting as godfather.

The next day, Vikings return to the town with Hastein in a coffin. They tell the bishop that Hastein died and that his final wish was to be buried in the cathedral with a proper Christian mass. The bishop is delighted to have converted a famous heathen, and allows fifty Vikings in mourning cloaks to carry the coffin into the cathedral. The whole town turns out to watch the spectacle.

When the bishop blesses Hastein's coffin with holy water and recites the passage about preparing for the dead to rise from their graves, Hastein bursts out of his coffin and cuts the bishop to pieces. His fifty Vikings throw off their cloaks, draw their long swords, and slaughter most of the town population. The Vikings fill their ships to the brim with loot and sail off into the Mediterranean.

Hastein spends his life raiding thousands of miles of coastline across dozens of kingdoms. He dies peacefully in his old age, with a pile of treasure. If you have lunch with him, don't let your guard down and keep one hand on your wallet.

THINGS VIKINGS LIKE TO DO

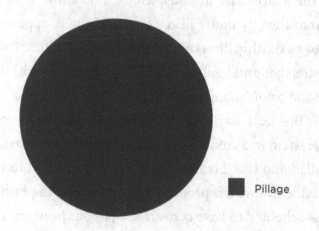

■ Pillage

Һеᒷρꝑuᒷ Һіᴎтs:
Һoᴡ то теᒷᒷ іꝼ уouꝛ ᴠіᒷᒷаgе іs іᴎꝼesтеᎅ ᴡітҺ ᴠіᴋіᴎgs

Not sure if your village is being raided by Vikings? Refer to this handy checklist!

1. Is your house on fire? ☐ Yes ☐ No ☐ Maybe

2. Is your village on fire? ☐ Yes ☐ No ☐ Maybe

3. Are you on fire? ☐ Yes ☐ No ☐ Maybe

4. Have your family and friends been carted off to Ireland to be sold in the Dublin slave markets?

☐ Yes ☐ No ☐ Maybe

5. Are your money, food, and livestock being hauled away by Vikings?

☐ Yes ☐ No ☐ Maybe

6. Is anyone in your village screaming, "Our village is infested with Vikings"?

☐ Yes ☐ No ☐ Maybe

7. Are you a Viking?

☐ Yes ☐ No ☐ Maybe

If you answered "yes" to three or more of these questions, your village may be infested with Vikings.

Viking Culture

The Vikings contribute more to Europe than just terror and mayhem. When they're not looting and pillaging, the Vikings are actually great traders, artists, craftsmen, and storytellers. They bring skiing to Europe, and are avid skaters as well. They worship many different gods: Tyr (called Tiw in England), the one-handed god of war, justice, and single combat; Odin (called Woden in England), the god of death and wisdom; Thor, the thunder god; and Frigg, the fertility goddess. These Viking gods are still honored by four of our days of the week*:

Sun's Day	Moon's Day	Tiw's Day	Woden's Day	Thor's Day	Frigg's Day	Saturn's Day
	Pillage! 1	Pillage! 2	Pillage! 3	Pillage! 4	Pillage! 5	Take a bath! 6
Pillage! 7	Pillage! 8	Pillage! 9	Pillage! 10	Pillage! 11	Pillage! 12	Take a bath! 13
Pillage! 14	Pillage! 15	Pillage! 16	Pillage! 17	Pillage! 18	Pillage! 19	Take a bath! 20
Pillage! 21	Pillage! 22	Pillage! 23	Pillage! 24	Pillage! 25	Pillage! 26	Take a bath! 27
Pillage! 28	Pillage! 29	Pillage! 30	Pillage! 31			

Viking Hygiene

Compared to much of Europe, Vikings are clean-freaks. They bathe at least once a week using a powerful soap made of lye and animal fat. Viking men will often bleach their hair blonder using the lye. Vikings also introduce the first proper combs to Europe. A Viking warrior is never without his beauty supplies, including brushes, tweezers, and even "ear spoons" for cleaning waxy ears.

* Saturn's Day is the only day still named for a Roman god, rather than a Viking god. The Viking word for Saturday is *lördag*, which means "washing day." It is the day for taking a bath.

Viking Law

Believe it or not, "law" is actually a Viking word. It is the Vikings who introduce England to the idea of trial by jury. The Vikings keep strict laws amongst themselves. Arsonists, appropriately enough, are burned at the stake. And if you kill your own brother you are hung upside down by your ankles next to a live wolf. If you cause a rebellion, you are tied to an angry bull.

Viking women enjoy more power than any other women in Europe. With their men away on raids, it is up to the women to run the households and even the towns. Both women and men have the right to divorce. And if a marriage lasts longer than twenty years before the divorce, the woman can keep half the property.

PEOPLE TO HAVE LUNCH WITH:
OLGA OF KIEV

Olga of Kiev is the Viking queen of Russia in the early 900s. Olga's husband, the king of Russia, is murdered by a non-Viking named Prince Mal. This Prince Mal character then has the nerve to ask Olga to marry him. He figures Olga will decide it is safer to be married to him than to resist him. Prince Mal figures wrong.

According to Time Corp records, Prince Mal sends

twenty of his chieftains to Olga to deliver his offer of marriage. Olga immediately has these men buried alive. She sends a message to Prince Mal saying she is flattered by his marriage offer, but insulted that he did not send all of his wisest and best noblemen to deliver the proposal.

Prince Mal eagerly sends every last one of his noblemen to Olga's castle. She gives them a warm welcome, inviting them to wash up in the bathhouse after their long journey. As soon as the noblemen pack into the bathhouse, Olga locks the doors, sets fire to the building, and burns Prince Mal's men alive.

Olga now rides to Prince Mal's castle with all of her soldiers. When she arrives at the gates, she explains to Prince Mal that she's so eager to accept his marriage proposal that she rode a few days ahead of the noblemen. This is an era before cell phones, so Prince Mal has no idea that Olga's been on a killing spree.

Prince Mal invites Olga and her soldiers inside for a huge feast. Olga quietly orders her men not to drink alcohol. After Prince Mal's soldiers are drunk, Olga's men kill over five thousand of them. They kill Prince Mal, too, while they're at it. Olga then places his entire city under siege.

She demands that each villager in the city deliver her three pigeons and three sparrows from each house. She says she doesn't ask for more because she doesn't want to impoverish the city. The villagers are thrilled with how kind Olga is, and each house delivers their birds to her.

At nightfall, Olga uses an old Viking trick. Her soldiers tie burning strips of cloth to each bird and release them. The terrified, flaming birds fly home to their nests in the eaves of the villagers' homes. Every building in town is set ablaze and Olga slaughters the townspeople as they try to flee the city gates.

If you do have lunch with Olga of Kiev, don't order the sparrow. And whatever you do, don't ask her to marry you.

MEANWHILE, IN THE AMERICAS

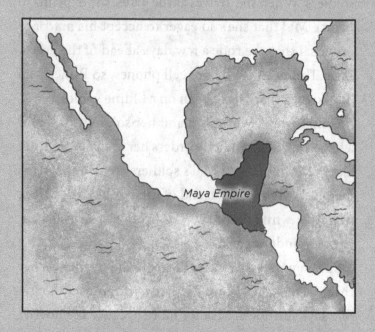

Maya Empire

The term "Middle Ages" only applies to European history, so you may be curious what the rest of the world is up to during this time period. If you have a sec, visit Central America in AD 900, when the Maya civilization is at its peak. The Maya build huge cities that are home to more than one hundred thousand people. They construct giant pyramids and temples and fill them with sculptures. They are excellent astronomers and develop a complex writing system. The Maya even build saunas for taking steam baths.

If you are hoping for an escape from all the violence going on over in Europe, just know that the Maya do practice human sacrifice. Other than that, you should have an excellent time there. Enjoy your visit!

The Vikings Get Civilized . . . Kind Of

So what can possibly stop the Vikings? Only one thing: they become so preposterously rich that they don't need to raid anyone anymore. The Vikings eventually end up with so much land and power, they simply settle down.

The French are completely *over* being attacked by Vikings all the time, and decide to just fork over much of their northern coast to the Viking "North Men." This new land is called

"Northmandy," or in French, "Normandy." It's a smart move for the French. Buffering their coast with Vikings stops other Viking raiders. The Viking newcomers get cozy in their new land, pick up the French language, and become nobility.

In 1066, one of the Vikings' descendants—a duke from Normandy named William—sets his sights on conquering England. For six hundred years, England has mostly* been ruled by a group of people called the Anglo-Saxons. But all that is about to end when William sails in and trounces the Anglo-Saxons at the Battle of Hastings.† Once the Normans rule England, they bring a new sense of law, order, and even French chivalry. Chivalry is a code of conduct practiced by rich warriors that encourages them to have good manners and good ethics, and not to raid and pillage like a bunch of Vikings.

The Viking age is now reaching its end. No longer nefarious pirates, the Vikings have looted and robbed their way to the throne. Vikings and their descendants rule Russia for centuries. They are kings in England and dukes in France. To strengthen alliances and trade with Europe, Vikings give up their pagan religion and become Christians. This newfound Christianity will soon draw Europe into more wars than ever before.

....

* Starting in AD 865, Vikings begin chipping away at England pretty relentlessly.

† The Battle of Hastings is actually fought at the town of Battle, which is northwest of Hastings, and was named Battle after the battle. So if any Normans ever start another battle there, it will be called the Battle of Battle. More interestingly, the Battle of Hastings is started by a juggler named Taillefer. William the Conqueror's personal jester, Taillefer stands in the middle of the battlefield and dazzles everyone by juggling his sword. An Anglo-Saxon finally attacks him. Taillefer slaughters his attacker before charging into the enemy line, single-handedly launching the battle.

PEOPLE TO HAVE LUNCH WITH:
WILLIAM THE CONQUEROR

Born in Normandy, France, in 1028, William is originally called William the Bastard because he is born to an unmarried mother. He quickly sets out to earn a better nickname. Not content to become "William the Baker," or "William the Wedding Dance Teacher," William up and takes over England, becoming "William the Conqueror."

He ends up killing as many as one hundred thousand English people either through warfare or by famine when he destroys the crops of his rebellious subjects. On the upside, he ends slavery. Before William's invasion, between 10 and 30 percent of England's people are slaves, and it is not considered a crime to beat or even kill them. So William really improves the lives of many of the English people that he doesn't murder or starve to death.

William the Conqueror brings taxation to England in a major way. This means English people get last names for the first time in their history, so William can keep better tax records.* With all that sweet,

* If people in your village call you Thomas, the son of John, your name might become Thomas Johnson. Or, if your name is Paul, and you're the town miller who grinds grain to make flour, you might become Paul Miller. If, however, people call you Bob Nosepicker, you probably have only yourself to blame.

sweet tax money, he is able to build castles—lots of castles. Before William's reign, England has zero castles—just wood-fortified towns. But by his death in 1087, nearly five hundred castles are built across England. The castles help keep his conquered people in line, as well as providing fancy digs for William's favorite knights and noblemen.*

You are welcome to attend William the Conqueror's funeral, but we hear it does not go particularly well. Legend has it that as soon as William dies, his attendants loot all his belongings, stripping him nearly naked. Then his funeral ceremony at St. Stephen's Abbey in Normandy is interrupted by an angry villager shouting that the church was illegally built on his father's land. Lastly, William's body turns out to be too fat to fit in his stone coffin. When monks try to force him in, the dead body's bowels burst, filling the church with such a horrendous stench that all the mourners stampede out of the ceremony.

* For a tour of a medieval castle, stay tuned for page 93.

3

THE CRUSADES

THINGS YOU WILL NEED

1. A broadsword
2. A shield, preferably new
3. A horse without too many miles on it
4. A grim sense of determination
5. A lust for blood
6. A squire to pull your armor off after you're stabbed by a Saracen

THINGS YOU WILL NOT NEED

1. Common sense

CONGRATULATIONS! You've done what very few villagers have done: survived the Early Middle Ages. You are now in the High Middle Ages (1000–1300). Why is it called the High Middle Ages? Because Middle Middle Ages sounds weird.

The High Middle Ages are a time of relative stability in Europe, but only when compared to the horrors of the Early Middle Ages and the absolute terrors of the Late Middle Ages. The Europeans still manage to get themselves into trouble by inciting a long string of completely unnecessary wars known as . . .

The Crusades

Probably the best that can be said for the Crusades is that they seemed like a good idea at the time. By the High Middle Ages, Europe is united by the Christian religion called Catholicism. The Catholics like to make pilgrimages to a region called "the Holy Land"* to visit the sites where the events of the Christian Bible take place. The only problem is, the Holy Land is currently controlled by Muslims who are not particularly hospitable to Christian pilgrims. In fact, Muslims are attacking Europe's allies in Turkey and doing an excellent job of winning new territory. The Crusades are Europe's attempt to push back the Muslim invaders while snatching the Holy Land from them in the process.

....
* The Holy Land is in modern-day Israel.

Thousands of European knights saddle up and march off to battle. Invading a foreign country, launching an expensive war, and picking a fight with an advanced culture—what could possibly go wrong?

THE MIDDLE EAST AND THE EMPIRE OF THE TURKS, 1200s

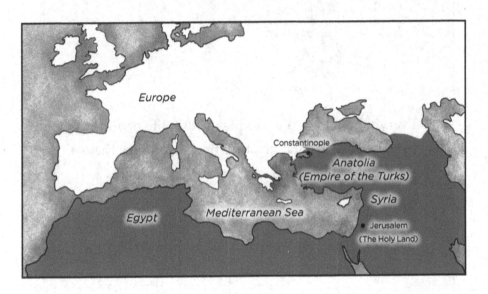

Helpful Hints:
Becoming a Knight

Everybody wants to be a knight. It's a life of adventure, derring-do, and great parties. Just follow these easy steps, and you too can join the knighthood.

1. Be Born Male. There are a few notable exceptions, but generally women aren't allowed to become knights. Sorry!

2. Be Born Rich. Buying weapons, armor, and a warhorse ain't cheap!

3. Become a Page. At age seven, you can become a page. You must go live with a knight and be his servant. You wash his clothes, clean his boots, serve his meals, and do whatever he asks. In exchange, he teaches you to fight. You do this for seven years until you become a squire.

4. Become a Squire. Congratulations! You are now a squire. You get to take care of the knight's horses, scrub his armor, and clean his weapons. You also have to accompany the knight into battle. In exchange, he'll keep teaching you to fight. You will do this for five or six years, or until you've had enough.

5. Become a Knight. If you're still alive, the knight can now promote you. First you'll have an all-night prayer vigil, and the next day you'll have your "dubbing ceremony." You will kneel before the knight, or a lord,* or even a king. They'll tap you on the shoulders with their sword. That's it! You are now a knight.

Alternative Path to Becoming a Knight: Be Heroic in Battle. If you don't want to spend fourteen years in training, there is a faster way to become a knight . . . but it is rare. If you fight as a regular foot soldier and perform exceptionally well in a battle, a lord can knight you on the spot. You just need to do something amazingly heroic to earn this honor. Consider using your iridium blaster to disintegrate an entire enemy army.

* A lord is a ruler over a large area of land. Finn Greenquill has tried to get Time Corp employees to start calling him Lord Greenquill, but it hasn't caught on yet.

The Pope and the Church

In 1095, Pope Urban II calls upon all the Christians in Europe to attack and conquer the Holy Land. A whole bunch of the Christians in Europe think about this and decide it's a great idea. They march to the Holy Land, massacre a bunch of surprised Muslims and Jewish people, and declare victory. Then most of the Christians pack up and return home to Europe. This exercise is known as the First Crusade.

You may be wondering, how can a pope be powerful enough to start a war?

In the Middle Ages, Europe is a cobb salad of nations, cultures, and peoples. Areas we now think of as, say, Belgium, Poland, or Italy are chopped up into zillions of tiny kingdoms and flavored with dozens of regional languages. Christianity is the zesty dressing that unites most of Europe. Even the pagan Vikings have been converted. This makes Christianity the most powerful force on the continent. And because the pope is in charge of Christianity, he is also the most powerful guy in Europe.

You may think of the pope as an elderly holy man with white robes and a big white hat. But in the Middle Ages, popes command armies.* The pope is a high church official elected by other high church officials to lead the Catholic Church. And once a pope is elected, he is pope for life. If Pope Urban II wants to start a war, it's as good as done.

....

* The pope's army is not disbanded until 1870.

Helpful Hints:
top five worst popes
in the middle ages

Some popes use their absolute power for good. Pope Leo I meets Attila the Hun in 452 and convinces him not to sack Rome. Pope Leo IX tries valiantly to keep the peace in the 1000s, though he does end up leading an army to attack southern Italy. Pope Alexander II protects Jewish people from being massacred in France, though he does order a crusade against the Moors in Spain. Suffice it to say, not all popes act like saints. Here are a few popes you may want to steer clear of.

1. Pope John XII (pope from 955 to 964) is not a model Christian. He blinds, dismembers, and murders his adversaries. He carries on many illegal affairs with young girls, including his own niece. He converts one of the pope's official palaces into a bar. He steals church offerings and—astonishingly for a pope—he makes toasts to the devil. He only stops when he is beaten to death by his mistress's husband.

2. Pope Benedict IX (pope from 1032 to 1044, 1045, and 1047 to 1048) commits many sordid crimes that

Finn Greenquill will not let us write about. In 1044, tired of being pope, Benedict sells his pope job to his godfather. In 1045 he returns to the job, only to leave one month later to marry his cousin. His parties become so excessive he is eventually thrown out of Rome.

3. Pope Alexander VI (pope from 1492 to 1503) becomes pope by bribing the right people. He quickly turns his pope job into a profitable gig by selling lucrative church jobs to his friends. When he needs more money, he falsely accuses rich people of crimes in order to seize their property. He then imprisons or murders his victims. So what does Alexander do with all this money? He throws insane parties with young children jumping out of cakes. Alexander goes on to father seven illegitimate kids.

4. Pope Stephen VI (pope from 896 to 897) hates his dead predecessor Pope Formosus so much that he orders Formosus's body dug out of the grave and put on trial. The pope's followers dutifully dig up the rotting nine-month-old corpse, dress him in papal vestments, and drag him into court. Not surprisingly, the corpse loses the trial. As punishment, three of Formosus's fingers are cut off. The corpse is then hauled through the streets and tossed in the Tiber River.

5. Pope Sergius III (pope from 904 to 911) is more of a mafia don than a pope. He orders several murders, including that of his predecessor Pope Leo V. Sergius's mistress is named Marozia. She and her mother, Theodora, are believed to be the wives, lovers, or assassins of half a dozen popes. Pulling strings, Marozia makes her son pope in 931.

PEOPLE TO HAVE LUNCH WITH:
ANNA KOMNENE

Anna Komnene is a Byzantine princess living in Constantinople.* She writes a valuable historical account of the First Crusade.

She is born on December 2, 1083, the first child of the Byzantine emperor. As soon as Anna is born, her marriage is already arranged. In the Middle Ages, people think this is perfectly normal. Anna spends her childhood getting a top-notch education in astronomy, medicine, history, geography, and math. In the Middle Ages, people think this is perfectly not normal. When she finally turns fourteen, she is

* Constantinople (today called Istanbul, in modern Turkey) is the capital of the Byzantine Empire. The Byzantines are descendants of the ancient Romans. Because they are Christian, they are loosely allied with Europe.

considered old enough to marry her fiancé, a thirty-five-year-old nobleman named Nicephorus. The marriage helps solidify her father's political power.

As an adult, Anna runs a hospital in Constantinople that houses ten thousand patients and orphans. There she teaches medicine and treats patients. After her husband dies, Anna enters a monastery and devotes her life to scholarship. Her fifteen-volume history of the Byzantine Empire contains the only surviving account of the First Crusade that is written from a Byzantine perspective.

MEANWHILE, IN ASIA . . .

Tired of all the wars in Europe? Wondering what's new in other parts of the world? Do yourself a favor and hop over to Southeast Asia to visit the Bagan Kingdom.

The 1100s are a time of enormous peace and prosperity in Bagan. The kingdom practices the Buddhist religion* and their national pastime is building magnificent temples. The capital city of Bagan is so wealthy, its inhabitants eventually build ten thousand temples

* Buddhism is a religion that starts in India in the sixth century BC. Whereas pagans believe in many gods, and Christians believe in just one god, Buddhists don't worship any god whatsoever. But this doesn't stop them from building incredible temples.

in a single valley. According to legend, the king of Bagan has a rare white elephant for a pet, and builds a temple wherever the elephant stops to take a nap. If you're feeling overwhelmed from fighting in the Crusades, a weekend getaway to Bagan may be just the thing you need.

A Whole Bunch of Other Crusades

There are nine major crusades and couple of minor ones over the course of two centuries. They all follow more or less the same pattern:

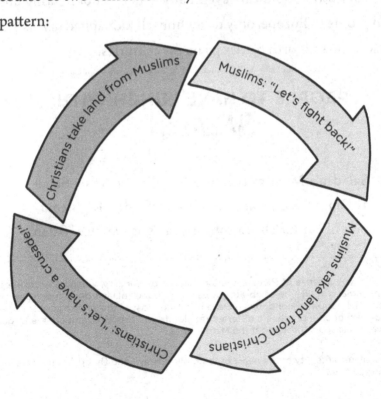

In 1174, a Muslim general named Saladin unites the Middle Eastern lands of Egypt and Syria. Saladin outfoxes and outfights the Europeans and successfully puts the Holy Land back in Muslim hands.

Richard the Lionheart, the king of England, joins the fight in the Third Crusade.* He fights Saladin to a draw, winning back much of the Holy Land. Richard installs his nephew Henry, the Count of Champagne, as the ruler of Jerusalem,† after the other ruler of Jerusalem is killed by Assassins. Henry likes his new job, but in 1197, while watching a parade, he accidentally falls out of his palace balcony. Adding insult to injury, his servant, a dwarf named Scarlet, tumbles out after Henry, landing on top of him. Both die.

Richard the Lionheart eventually gets tired of fighting and heads home to Europe, only to get himself kidnapped in Austria. These back-and-forth battles go on for centuries.

PEOPLE TO HAVE LUNCH WITH:
SALADIN

Saladin's Muslim title is Al-Malik Al-Nasir Salah al-Din, which means "Mighty Defender, Righteousness of Faith." The Europeans can't pronounce "Salah

---

* To give you a sense of Richard the Lionheart's personality, when he is crowned king of England in 1189, he celebrates by passing a bunch of laws persecuting Jewish people. The people of London celebrate by killing most of the Jewish people in the city. Jewish people practice a different religion from Christians, and are the target of awful massacres throughout the Middle Ages.

† Jerusalem is the city at the heart of the biblical Holy Land that the Crusaders are fighting to take.

al-Din" and so simply call him "Saladin."

Soldiering is Saladin's family business. His uncle is a famous general who helps Saladin rise through the military ranks until he finally commands an army. He fights battles for years in order to unite a Muslim army to destroy the Crusaders. The Assassins hate Saladin because, while he is a Muslim as they are, he follows a different branch of their religion. This will not do. The Assassins try to kill Saladin several times, though they never succeed.

At the end of his life, Saladin gives all his wealth to the poor. When he dies of fever on March 4, 1193, he has only one gold piece and forty pieces of silver, not enough to pay for his own funeral.

Helpful Hints:
assassins

The Assassins are a secretive sect of Muslims trained in the art of killing. Led by a shadowy leader from a mountain fortress in Persia, the Order of Assassins kills sultans,* viziers,† and Crusader knights for hundreds of years.

One reason the Assassins are so good at their jobs

* A sultan is the ruler of a Muslim state. A yardstick is the ruler of things longer than a foot.

† A vizier is a high-ranking official who serves a sultan, pharaoh, or king. A visor is the lid on your cap.

is that many are willing to die when carrying out an assignment. A European explorer named Marco Polo, whom you'll be introduced to in the next chapter, says the Assassins believe they will go to heaven if they are killed on the battlefield.

Word to the wise: if you meet any shady characters in your travels, just be friendly. You don't want to end up on an Assassin hit list.

The Children's Crusade

Perhaps the weirdest and saddest crusade is called the Children's Crusade.*

In the year 1212, a twelve-year-old shepherd boy named Stephen of Cloyes believes God has ordered him to lead the children of Europe to rid the Holy Land of Muslims. Stephen begins preaching, and a shocking number of kids take him seriously. He soon amasses a following of thirty thousand children.

Stephen leads his groupies south. Not only have these kids left their homes, a lot of them freeze or starve to death on the long hike over the mountainous Alps. Only one in three kids survives

---

* The facts of the Children's Crusade are a little sketchy. We've written a fairly traditional version of the story. Let Time Corp know if you find out exactly what happened. Just try not to get yourself sold to the Tunisians!

the trek to Italy. When they finally reach the Mediterranean Sea, Stephen tells his followers that God will part the sea and allow them to march all the way to the Holy Land. Unfortunately, the sea does not part.

In a word: awkward.

Some of the children attempt to march into the Mediterranean Sea and promptly drown. Two enterprising merchants, Hugh the Iron and William the Pig, offer to ferry the rest of the kids on their boats for free. When the kids accept the free boat rides to the Holy Land, Hugh and William sail the children to Tunisia instead and sell them into slavery. This is a good example of why you shouldn't accept rides from strangers.

PEOPLE TO HAVE LUNCH WITH:
HILDEGARD OF BINGEN

Hildegard of Bingen is one of the smartest people in medieval times. She enters a nunnery* when she is fifteen and devotes her life to science, research, and Christian worship. When she turns thirty-eight, her fellow nuns elect her to run the nunnery.† Hildegard eventually founds two additional nunneries nearby.

* A nunnery is a place where women go to live to devote their lives to Christianity. Nuns often take vows of poverty, perform services for the poor, and do not marry. A monastery is basically the same thing, except it's for men.

† Hildegard of Bingen is one of the few people in history who can truly be said to be a jack-of-all-trades, master of nuns.

In the High Middle Ages, monasteries and nunneries are still the best places to find books and receive an education. Hildegard takes great advantage of this. She is a prolific writer, composer, poet, and philosopher. Much of what modern historians know about medieval music comes from studying Hildegard's many compositions. She also writes several books about medicine and science.

At a time in history when women have very few rights and opportunities, Hildegard becomes a respected scholar. Important church officials seek out her opinion on difficult questions. Hildegard lives to the ripe old age of eighty-one and is eventually recognized as a saint by the Catholic Church.

HeLpfuL HiNts:
tHe kNigHts templaR

If becoming an Assassin is not your speed, you may be interested in joining the Knights Templar. They are an order of Christian knights that forms during the Crusades. Their duty is to take the Holy Land from the Muslims and to protect Christian travelers making pilgrimages there.

As part of their services, the Templars open up lending banks along the pilgrimage routes to the Holy Land. These banks make the Templars fantastically wealthy. King Philip IV of France winds up deeply in debt to the Templars. So he cooks up a brilliant way to become debt-free. On Friday, October 13, 1307, he orders his army to arrest the Templar leaders and burn them at the stake. Problem solved! No more Templars. Some believe this massacre is the reason people consider Friday the thirteenth to be an unlucky day.

Enough with the Crusades, Already

Europe's appetite for crusades peters out by the end of the Middle Ages. A lot of blood has been spilled, and not much land has been gained. Some of the crusades are disasters of galactic proportions. The Fourth Crusade, for instance, results in overenthusiastic knights sacking Constantinople, a city that is both Christian and kind of an ally.

The Crusades do open up trade routes and some idea exchanges with the Middle East. But they probably cause far too many massacres to be worth this prize. If you're fed up with the countries of Europe bullying other nations in the Crusades, then you'll love the next leg of your journey. Europe is about to be pummeled by the biggest bully in world history. . . .

4

GENGHIS KHAN AND THE MONGOL EMPIRE

THINGS YOU WILL NEED

1. A fast horse
2. A good bow with sixty arrows
3. A healthy appetite for sheep's brains and dried marmot

THINGS YOU WILL NOT NEED

1. Laundry detergent
2. A conscience

In 1241, while Europe is still messing around with crusades, new invaders arrive that catch Europe with its pants down. These invaders are more terrifying and powerful than any that have come before. Their very name strikes terror into the hearts of people across an entire continent. They are the Mongols, and they are coming to kill everyone.

The Mongols have ravaged China, destroyed central Asia, and burned much of Russia to the ground. They have massacred millions. Remember the deadly Assassins from the Crusades? All killed. Remember the peaceful kingdom of Bagan? Its king was chased out of the country. The Mongols are as unstoppable as a hurricane. And now they are galloping into Europe.

Who is this fearsome enemy? Where did they come from? It all starts with a man named Genghis Khan.

EARLY MONGOL AND KHWARAZMIAN EMPIRES, 1206

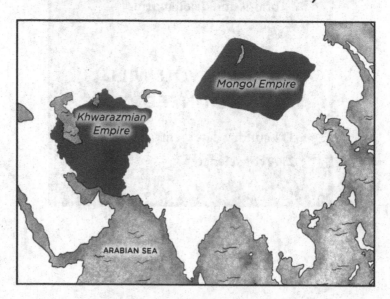

Genghis Khan

Set your time machine to Mongolia in 1171 and you will meet a nine-year-old named Temüjin. He's just been sent to meet his future wife and live with her tribe. The boy may not look like much, but he's going to grow up to build the largest land empire in history. And he will take on the title "Universal Ruler," or, as he is more famously known, "Genghis Khan."

You may think you've had a rough childhood, but you probably haven't had a childhood like Genghis Khan's. Like all Mongol children, Genghis is tied to a horse's saddle at age three in order to learn to ride. He's taught to sleep in the saddle and ride for days without food.

Genghis doesn't get along with his big brother, so he murders him. Imagine being this kid's babysitter! When his father is poisoned by a rival tribe, Genghis is captured and thrown into slavery. He soon escapes into the wilderness and stays alive by eating ox carcasses and marmots. He gets married at age sixteen, but his wife is quickly captured by an enemy tribe and sold into slavery herself. Genghis goes and steals her back. This is his childhood.

All this is a long way of saying, Genghis Khan is one tough dude. By the time he's a teenager, he is a feared and respected warrior, proven on the battlefield. By age twenty-four, he's elected khan of the Mongols.

A Mongol Warrior

Genghis Attacks China

Genghis's Mongol army starts brutalizing China in 1206, massacring millions and looting a fortune in treasure. When the Mongols eventually destroy the Chinese city of Beijing, sixty thousand Chinese women are said to leap from the city walls to their deaths rather than be captured alive and tortured by the dreaded Mongols. The Mongols stack towers of Chinese bones so high, travelers crossing the plains compare them to snowcapped mountains.

Genghis Obliterates the Khwarazmian Empire

The Khwarazmian Empire includes modern-day Iran and much of the Middle East. Its governor, Inalchuq, did not get the memo about treating Genghis Khan with respect. When Genghis sends a caravan of 450 Mongol traders to Khwarazm, the Khwarazmians kill the traders and steal their cargo. When Genghis sends ambassadors to Khwarazm for an apology, Inalchuq chops off an ambassador's head and ships it back to Mongolia.

Genghis Khan is not a guy to be laid-back about this type of thing. He is unamused.

He amasses his army and utterly destroys Khwarazm. The population plummets by as many as ten million people. The Mongols are said to kill 1.2 million people in the city of Urgench alone.* They stack up towers of skulls around the city. When Genghis finally captures Inalchuq, he kills him by pouring molten silver into his eyes and ears.

Buh-Bye, Russia

The Mongols sweep across Russia. They don't want to leave enemies at their back, so they kill everyone they encounter. This is why the Mongols create such a high death toll. Remember those fierce Vikings who ruled Russia from the city of Kiev? Of Kiev's fifty thousand citizens, only two thousand survive.

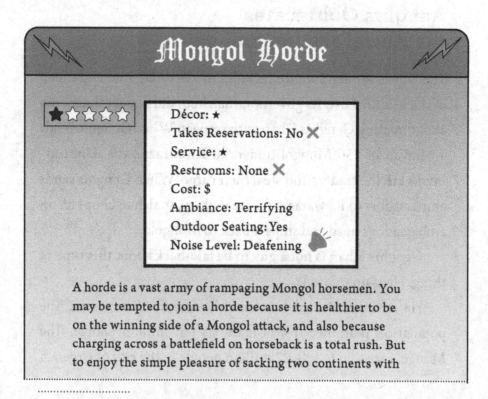

Mongol Horde

★☆☆☆☆

Décor: ★
Takes Reservations: No ✕
Service: ★
Restrooms: None ✕
Cost: $
Ambiance: Terrifying
Outdoor Seating: Yes
Noise Level: Deafening

A horde is a vast army of rampaging Mongol horsemen. You may be tempted to join a horde because it is healthier to be on the winning side of a Mongol attack, and also because charging across a battlefield on horseback is a total rush. But to enjoy the simple pleasure of sacking two continents with

* How is this accomplished? All of Genghis's fifty thousand soldiers are commanded to kill twenty-four people each.

Genghis Khan's army, you'll need to be in pretty good shape and not too squeamish about killing millions of people.

Each warrior leads four horses so he always has a fresh mount. This way, a horseman can ride all day without stopping. Mongol riders prick their horses in the neck with a knife and drink the blood,* just to save themselves the hassle of pausing to fill up their water canteens.[†] In this way, the Mongols can cross hundreds of miles in a week, surprising and surrounding every army they encounter.

If you want to be a Mongol horse archer, you'd better start practicing. For better aim, Mongols are trained to fire their arrows while all four of their horse's hooves are off the ground. Each Mongol carries sixty arrows in their quiver and fires at least twelve arrows per minute. A good-size horde can fill the air with fifty thousand arrows inside sixty seconds.[‡]

One downside of joining the Mongol horde is the smell. A Mongol will cross the entire Asian continent without once thinking to wash his shirt. It is said you can smell the horde coming hours before it actually arrives.

The Mongols are so unclean, they may even have spread the Black Plague to Europe.[§] They accomplish this by

....

* Gives a whole new meaning to the word "bloodthirsty."

† Don't complain about drinking blood. When Mongols run out of horse blood, they're not afraid to snack on dogs or rats. When they run out of rats, Mongols will kill every tenth soldier in the horde and eat him. Seriously.

‡ People become so terrified of Mongols, they are often afraid to fight. In one account, a Mongol warrior is about to execute some villagers when he realizes he forgot his ax. He orders the townspeople to wait for him while he fetches his weapon. They sit patiently until he returns and chops them to pieces.

§ See Chapter 7 for more information than you ever wanted to know about the Black Plague.

catapulting infected dead bodies into cities they surround, in order to kill off the inhabitants.

Here is what some of our readers say about the Mongol horde:

★ "I should have joined the Mongol horde."
—Anna V., Kiev

★★★★ "Has anyone seen my ax?" —Batu, Mongol warrior

Just How Bad Was Genghis?

By now you've probably figured out that Genghis Khan is not a man you want to ask to borrow a cup of sugar. But just how bad is he?

GENGHIS KHAN
PROS AND CONS

Pros

✘ Outlaws selling Mongolian women into forced marriages

✘ Outlaws theft

✘ Lowers taxes

✘ Mostly allows people to practice whichever religion they want

Cons

✘ Creates an army that kills forty million people. That's 11 percent of the world population in AD 1200.

✘ Slaughters so many farmers that it changes the world. Thousands of abandoned farms grow back into forests all over Russia and Asia. Scientists believe this reforestation scrubs seven hundred million tons of carbon dioxide from the atmosphere.*

✘ Fathers a ridiculous number of children. Today, sixteen million men worldwide are descended from Genghis Khan.†

....

* Since this helps the environment, some could argue this is a pro, not a con. By allowing millions of miles of forests to regrow, Genghis Khan may be the ultimate environmentalist.

† To be fair, this is par for the course for world rulers. Remember William the Conqueror? Twenty-five percent of England is descended from him.

LARGEST EMPIRES IN HISTORY
(BY PERCENTAGE OF THE EARTH'S LAND AREA)

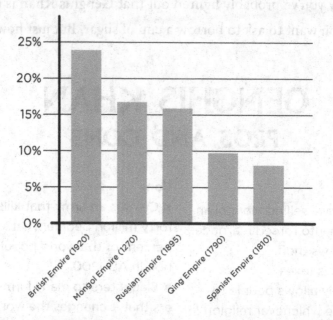

The Mongols build the largest empire in premodern history. Seven hundred years later, only the British will succeed in building a larger empire.

HeLpfuL HiNts:
gift ideas for genghis khan

Some countries avoid destruction by sending money to the Mongols. Korea, for instance, gets tired of being burned to the ground and instead agrees to pay the Mongols ten thousand otter skins, twenty thousand horses, ten thousand bolts of silk, one million soldier uniforms, and a large number of child slaves.

If you want to save a country from ruin, you'll have to think of a good gift to impress Genghis Khan. But what to get for the man who has everything?

Luckily, you're a time traveler. So you have a lot of options. Here are . . .

TIME CORP'S TOP TEN
GIFT IDEAS FOR GENGHIS KHAN

10. A yoga membership
9. A water bottle, so he doesn't have to drink horse blood
8. A babysitting service to help with his two thousand kids
7. Google Maps
6. Deodorant, but be subtle about it
5. A therapist. He clearly has anger issues.
4. A five-dollar gift certificate to the Time Corp souvenir shop*
3. A Toyota Camry. He must be sick of riding a horse by now.
2. A bath
1. A one-way ticket to the last ice age

* Now available from Time Corp for only ten dollars!

The Mongol Invasion of Europe

After toppling Russia, the Mongols invade Europe with three armies. Set your time machine for 1241 and set your expectations high. You will need strong armor and a strong stomach: the Mongols are about to kill another couple million people.

They pummel Poland, blast Bohemia, and crush Croatia. When they reach Hungary, they obliterate a quarter of the population, including an army of the Knights Templar. Now almost nothing stands in the way of the Mongols destroying all of Europe. What are the Mongols' motives? Sure, their empire is enormous, but as Finn Greenquill can tell you, an empire can always get bigger....

PRANKING THE PAST

Always sacking cities and burning villages, Mongols are almost no fun at all. Follow these easy steps to lighten the mood in the Mongol army:

1. Find a rampaging Mongol horde attacking a city. This should be easy enough in the 1200s.
2. Use your Time Corp Time Travel Device™ to freeze time.
3. Replace all of the Mongols' bows with ping-pong paddles.
4. Replace all their arrows with ping-pong balls.
5. Restart time and enjoy the battle!

The Mongol Legacy

It's 1242 and the Mongol horde is poised to flatten Europe. The Europeans need a miracle, and they get one. The khan, ruling from Mongolia, dies after drinking too much on a hunting trip. All his generals must race back to Mongolia to make their claims to be the next khan.

The Mongol armies, on the verge of trampling Europe, vanish overnight. They gallop with all haste back to Asia, never to return.

Europe is spared . . . kind of. The Mongols helped to spread a disease that will bring the continent to its knees: the Black Death. But that is a story for another chapter.

PEOPLE TO HAVE LUNCH WITH:
MARCO POLO

Marco Polo is an Italian merchant and adventurer who travels across Asia and writes the first European account of China and the Mongol Empire.

Marco is born in 1254, the son of a wealthy trader, Niccolò Polo. Marco's mom dies when he is young, so he is raised by his aunt and uncle. He does not meet his dad until he is sixteen, when his father returns from a long trading journey.

Kublai Khan, the grandson of Genghis Khan, now rules the eastern lands of the Mongol Empire. He tasks Marco's father with delivering one hundred Christian scholars to the Mongol court, as well as oil from the holy city of Jerusalem.

Niccolò takes eighteen-year-old Marco on his journey to China to meet the great khan.

First they sail to the Holy Land to grab some holy oil. Next they ride camels to what is now modern-day Iran and follow the trade routes east. Their caravan is attacked by bandits in a sandstorm, but they manage to escape. After three years on the march, they finally reach the khan's summer palace in Shangdu, China.* There, the Polos spend many years in the khan's court. Their journey home from China by sea is incredibly dangerous. Of the six hundred people traveling in their convoy, only eighteen survive the trip back to Iran. From Iran, the Polos trek up to the Black Sea and sail home to Venice, Italy.

By the time Marco returns to Venice in 1295, he has traveled for twenty-four years, crossing fifteen thousand miles and amassing a fortune in gemstones. Rather than simply retiring, Marco joins Venice's war against the neighboring city-state of Genoa. He is soon captured and imprisoned in 1296. Marco is lucky enough to share his prison cell with a professional writer, who writes down all of Marco's stories into a book, *The Travels of Marco Polo*. The book becomes extremely popular across Europe, and will eventually inspire a young explorer named Christopher Columbus to try to find a faster route to Asia by sea.

Marco is released after three years in prison and goes on to make an even larger fortune as a merchant. After several successful decades of trading, he dies on January 8, 1324, at the age of seventy. If you take Marco out to lunch, let him pick up the check—he can afford it.

* The palace is also known as Xanadu. Kublai Khan's summer palace is rumored to be so incredibly fancy, it's even nicer than Finn Greenquill's summer palace. If you can find a way to spend a night in Xanadu, we highly recommend it!

5

A JOUSTING TOURNAMENT

THINGS YOU WILL NEED

1. A good horse
2. A suit of armor or your fanciest clothes
3. A strong lance
4. A high pain tolerance
5. Some aspirin

All right, all right, fine. We know you didn't buy Time Corp's expensive Middle Ages travel package just to get yourself pillaged by Vikings and sacked by a Mongol horde. You forked over your hard-earned dollars for the glamor and fun of medieval times: the lavish banquets, the impressive castles, the fine lords and ladies, the exciting jousts and melees, the gallant knights on quests, and the attractively affordable hotel options.

Crossing the world with Genghis Khan's army is thirsty, tiring work, and you deserve a flagon of cider and a day off. So steer your time machine for the nearest castle; it's time to visit a proper medieval party, otherwise known as . . .

A Royal Progress

A royal progress is when a medieval ruler travels across their realm in a grand procession, popping in at the local towns and castles, and making sure everything's running smoothly.* Each time the king, queen, prince, or princess reaches a town, the town throws them the biggest party it can manage. So if you can weasel your way into a royal entourage that is touring the country, your life will become pretty much one nonstop party.

The town leaders from the local government, the church, and even the university (if there is one) will greet your royal procession outside the town walls and present you with a ceremonial key to the city. With a fanfare of trumpets, you will enter the town gates to find the city streets decorated with colorful tapestries and canopies for your grand parade. Some towns go to enormous lengths to impress their guests, even dressing up herds of bulls in costumes, draping them in bright cloth, and hanging bells from their horns . . . because nothing says "welcome" like a well-decorated bull.

....
* Finn Greenquill performs a royal progress around Time Corp headquarters twice a week.

The Market

In the heart of every medieval town, you will find a market. And with a royal progress passing through, the market will be jam-packed. Spice sellers hawk pepper and nutmeg and even cinnamon from Arab trade routes to the east. The tanners, trappers, and clothiers sell wool, furs, and cured hides. The fishmonger might try to mong you some fish. Merchants might offer you bargains on linen, canvas, and even silk.*

The butcher will sell you a decent cut of fresh goat, sheep, or pig. If he makes the mistake of selling anyone rotten meat, townspeople will force him to eat the rotten meat and then lock him in the pillory. If the vintner sells you bad wine, he will be forced to drink some of the wine, be locked in the pillory, and then have the rest of his bad wine dumped on his head.

* The silk is imported mostly from China. The trade routes that bring silk all the way to Europe from China are owed, at least in part, to the Mongol conquest.

HeLpfuL HiNts:
BearBaitiNg

If you are starved for entertainment, and not in the mood for shopping at the market, you can always attend a bearbaiting. Bearbaiting is extremely popular in England in the Middle Ages and involves a captured bear being tied to a stake and then attacked by vicious dogs. If this doesn't sound entertaining enough for you, you can always attend a bullbaiting, which is exactly the same thing except with a male cow.* The English will basically pit any two animals against each other if they think it will sell tickets. At one baiting in London, an ape is tied to a pony's back and set upon by dogs. If this sport strikes you as unnecessarily cruel, just remember that medieval people did not yet have reality TV to keep themselves entertained.†

Compete in a Tournament

To celebrate the royal progress, there's a decent chance your local lord will host a tournament—a thrilling event where knights

* Bulldogs are bred specifically for bullbaiting. Bullbaiting remains hugely popular in England all the way up until it is banned in 1835. Bulldogs are out of a job after 1835, but have stayed popular as house pets.

† This entire sidebar is so tasteless, it could be served for lunch in the Time Corp employee cafeteria.

compete for honor and prizes. Tournaments are hugely popular. A big tournament in France might attract competing knights from England, Scotland, Spain, Germany, and even Italy. More than three thousand knights attend a French tournament in November 1179 to celebrate King Philip II's coronation.

One big tournament event is jousting, where knights buckle on suits of armor, heft up twelve-foot lances, and charge at each other on horseback. The goal is to knock your opponent off his horse. Since you've just crossed the Russian steppe with Genghis Khan's horde, you're probably a little saddle sore. Jumping right back on a horse may not be at the top of your wish list. Still, it's safer than joining in the main event at a tournament: the melee.

RESULTS IF YOU FIGHT IN A MELEE

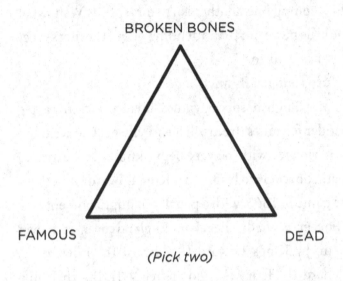

BROKEN BONES

FAMOUS   DEAD

(Pick two)

In the melee, a bunch of knights might be left in an arena to fight one another until there's only one knight left standing. Sometimes your weapons are blunted, to keep from killing your fellow competitors. But not always. It's no surprise that a lot of knights are killed in these melees. So why sign up for this treatment? Oh, no real reason, just tons of money, fame, and honor. Some knights become fantastically wealthy by winning tournaments. William Marshal, First Earl of Pembroke, is considered to be the best tournament knight of all time. Over the course of his career, he goes from rags to riches. According to the earl himself, he bests more than five hundred knights in tournaments.

Helpful Hints:
Soccer

Need a break from the melee? Maybe knights bludgeoning one another isn't your speed? Well, what could be more fun than attending one of the first soccer matches in history?

Turns out, nearly anything.

Early English soccer games involve kicking a pig bladder for miles, from village to village. Games often turn violent, with players being knifed or beaten to death. Soccer is so brutal that King Edward III outlaws the game in 1363, with a penalty of imprisonment.*

Soccer is made illegal in England over and over again, by Kings Edward II, Edward III, Edward IV, Richard II, Henry IV, and Henry VIII. But the game is just too popular to go away. Today soccer is played in every country in the world, and very few players are beaten to death.

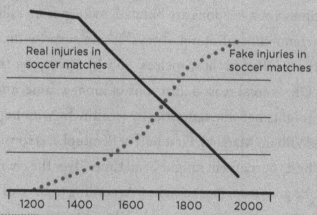

Real injuries in soccer matches

Fake injuries in soccer matches

1200   1400   1600   1800   2000

* King Edward III may have been partly motivated to ban soccer because he wanted people to spend more time practicing archery.

A Feast at the Castle

If you've won any of the events in the tournament, your prizes will be presented at a fancy dinner in the local lord's castle. Whether you've won or not, you've probably worked up an appetite, what with all the jousting and melees and bearbaiting. So don your finest tunic or your most elegant gown: it's time to attend a medieval feast.

Dinner is served in the great hall of the castle. This is a massive room with a high, vaulted ceiling. The walls are stone and hung with tapestries, coats of arms,* and animal trophies. The room is heated with fireplaces so large you can stand in them, though we don't recommend you try this. The lord of the castle and his most honored guests eat at the "high table" that sits on a raised platform at one end of the room. If the lord is wealthy, the serving platters will be made of silver and gold.†

Jugglers and jesters entertain the guests. Musicians play lutes, flutes, harps, and guitars. In the Early Middle Ages, you tried pottage, the staple food of poor villagers. But now you are getting some fine dining in a big castle. Food is served buffet-style and it's all-you-can-eat. So fill up your plate!

---

* A coat of arms is an insignia that a noble family puts on their shields, flags, or uniforms. Finn Greenquill's coat of arms features a hyena stealing a bag of money from a baby.

† Don't try to filch any; there are guards everywhere. Finn Greenquill learned this lesson the hard way.

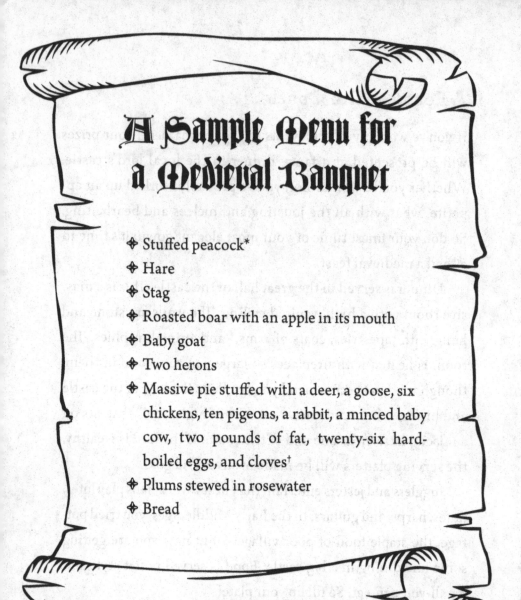

A Sample Menu for a Medieval Banquet

+ Stuffed peacock*
+ Hare
+ Stag
+ Roasted boar with an apple in its mouth
+ Baby goat
+ Two herons
+ Massive pie stuffed with a deer, a goose, six
  chickens, ten pigeons, a rabbit, a minced baby
  cow, two pounds of fat, twenty-six hard-
  boiled eggs, and cloves†
+ Plums stewed in rosewater
+ Bread

....

* The peacock is stuffed, and you will be, too, if you try to eat it all.

† To this day, Europeans are very open-minded about what you can call a "pie."

QUICK ETIQUETTE TIPS!

- Don't start eating until the lord has taken his first bite.
- Forks haven't been invented yet. You can use a knife and spoon, or just eat with your hands. Another option is to use a trencher of stale bread as a bowl.
- Unless you are the lord, you have to bring your own knife, spoon, and cup to dinner.
- If you forget to bring a cup, you need to share out of the communal cup. It has a bunch of handles so anyone at your table can grab it and take a gulp.

Tour the Castle

Unless you have a really high tolerance for lute music and heron meat, you're probably ready for a tour of the castle. Slip out of the great hall and you may find yourself in the bailey, the courtyard in the middle of the castle. The lord probably sleeps up in the keep, the highest tower in the castle. Soldiers, blacksmiths, stable hands, and kitchen staff sleep in smaller buildings around the castle. Somewhere deep in the basement is the dungeon. You may want to steer clear: it's probably filled with a nasty amount of torture equipment.

A MEDIEVAL CASTLE

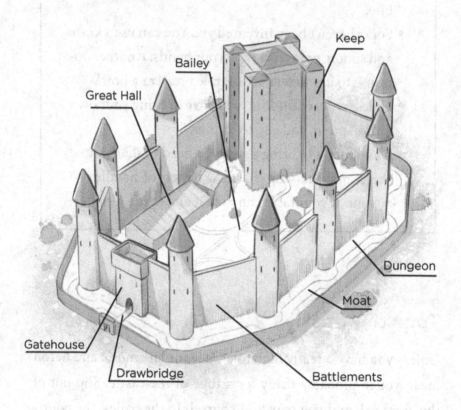

Great Hall · Bailey · Keep · Dungeon · Moat · Battlements · Drawbridge · Gatehouse

Wandering the castle, you'll find it is designed for defense more than comfort. In the Middle Ages, you never know who is going to invade you: it could be Moors, it could be neighboring lords, or it could be your own family members. This is why all the walls are fitted with arrow loops—slits for archers shooting arrows. This makes the castle awfully drafty, and aside from the occasional fireplace, there is no central heating.

CROSS SECTION OF CASTLE GATEHOUSE

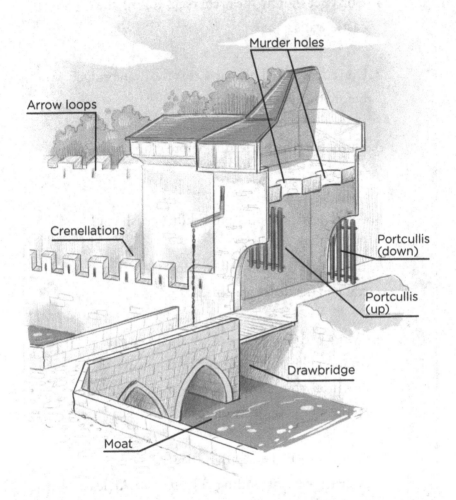

Murder holes

Arrow loops

Crenellations

Portcullis (down)

Portcullis (up)

Drawbridge

Moat

The only way in and out of a castle is through the main gatehouse. If you try to invade a castle through the front gates, you'll have a long checklist of defenses to pass before you make it inside.

Helpful Hints:
How to Storm a Castle

1. Don't get shot by the archers patrolling the castle walls.

2. Don't drown in the moat. Cross the drawbridge before the defenders can raise it.

3. Sprint past the portcullis before it drops down on you.

4. Good news: the portcullis didn't crush you!

5. Bad news: the portcullis is now shut. You are trapped inside the gatehouse.

6. More bad news: the ceiling is filled with "murder holes." Defenders are hurling rocks down on you. Now might be a good time to reconsider your decision to storm this castle.

7. Okay, more bad news: defenders are now pouring vats of boiling oil on you. At least you're getting a warm welcome.

8. You probably don't want any more bad news right now. So just pretend that archers are not

firing arrows at you through arrow loops in the gatehouse walls.

9. All right, there's more bad news: your Time Corp vacation bill just arrived and it's enormous.

10. Sorry you didn't succeed in storming the castle. Better luck next time!

Tour the Local Cathedral

Religion may slaughter a lot of innocent people in the Middle Ages, but it inspires some pretty nifty art. If it's not too late at night, you may want to slip out and visit the local cathedral. Once medieval builders unlock the secrets of Roman cement, they begin building with a vengeance. The spire of the Lincoln Cathedral in England stands taller than the great pyramids of

Egypt. The Aachen Cathedral in Germany has stained-glass windows eighty-four feet high. The Sedlec Abbey in Bohemia is not particularly big, but you may be curious to visit the abbey's small underground chapel: it's decorated with the skeletons of more than forty thousand people.

Christianity is not the only religion to inspire great architecture. If you have time, be sure to check out the Jewish Synagogue of Tomar in Portugal, with its grand pillars and vaulted ceiling. The Muslim Great Mosque of Córdoba is also worth a visit, though if you pop in anytime after 1236, you will find it has been turned into a Catholic cathedral.

If you're tired of visiting cathedrals and gorging yourself at medieval banquets, then get excited: your next adventure will include absolutely zero cathedrals, and plenty of chances to burn off a few calories—when you are running for your life. . . .

6

THE HUNDRED YEARS' WAR

So much for the High Middle Ages. You have now survived to the Late Middle Ages. The good news is you are just a few hundred years from the age of reason, clean drinking water, and a germ theory of disease. The bad news is the Late Middle Ages are a period of famine, plague, uprisings, and incredibly long wars. How incredibly long? Well, one of them is called the Hundred Years' War.

The first thing that can be said about the Hundred Years' War is that it doesn't last one hundred years. Like most things in the

Middle Ages, it is actually much worse. It lasts 116 years, from 1337 to 1453.

Ever since William the Conqueror left France to claim dibs on England, the English king has owned land on both sides of the English Channel. As centuries pass, it becomes really murky how much land belongs to the English king versus the French king. Topping it off, both men have legitimate claims to be the king of France.

In 1337, the French king begins seizing land from the English. Adding insult to injury, the French team up with the Scottish, form a huge fleet of warships, and threaten a massive invasion on the English coast. The king of England decides enough is enough. He attacks the fleet and destroys it. And thus begins the great English and French pastime: going to war with each other.

HeLpfuL HiNts:
fasHioN tips foR tHe Late midDLe ages

If you're going to travel to the Late Middle Ages, you might as well travel in style. Here are two quick tips:

GENTLEMEN
Clown shoes are the height of fashion. Starting in the 1330s, long-toed shoes are *en vogue*. The longer the shoe, the better. By the late 1300s, shoe toes are

so long, they must be reinforced with whalebone. Noblemen start tying the ends of their shoes to their leggings in order to shuffle around. Crusader knights are forced to chop the toes of their shoes off in order to flee an enemy.

LADIES

In the Late Middle Ages, it's extremely fashionable to pluck off your entire eyebrows and cut off all your eyelashes. This draws more attention to your forehead, which is considered the height of beauty.*

---

* Time Corp's legal department insists this is not a prank to see if you will shave your eyebrows. This is *actually* what men and women find attractive in the Late Middle Ages.

The Battle of Crécy

Time travel to Crécy, France, on August 26, 1346, to witness one of the more lopsided and impressive military victories of history. The English are badly outnumbered by the French, who want them out of their country. The French have at least 30,000 soldiers, including at least 1,500 knights in plate armor, mounted on warhorses. When the French take the battlefield, they raise a red flag in the air that means they will take no prisoners. It's a bad time to be an Englishman. . . .

The English have fewer than half as many soldiers as the French. But they have one important weapon: the English longbow. This powerful weapon kills from two hundred yards: that's two football fields. The longbow proves too much for the French, who are pulverized. This battle marks a turning point in European warfare. A snooty nobleman with expensive armor, a warhorse, and a lifetime of jousting experience can now be beaten by a mere peasant with a bow and arrow.

THE ENGLISH LONGBOW

If you want to try your hand at this impressive weapon, you need to start young. English boys are given their first bows as early as six. As boys grow older and stronger, they are given heavier bows. By the time they're adults, English bowmen use six-foot yew bows with a 150-pound draw weight. What does this mean? Picture lifting a 150-pound adult off the ground with one hand. That's how strong you need to be to draw an English longbow.

When Frenchmen find English longbows on the battlefield, they simply do not have the muscles to draw them. So the weapon is useless when it falls into enemy hands. To ensure a large talent pool of English archers, King Edward III passes the Archery Law of 1363, commanding all Englishmen to practice archery for two hours every Sunday after church. English archers carry between sixty and seventy-two arrows and are insanely accurate shots because they've practiced their whole lives. A longbow can pierce armor and kill a warhorse. It's a pretty handy weapon to have in a pinch.

Feudalism

How are the French and English kings able to cobble together so many thousands of soldiers to fight their never-ending wars? To even attempt this might seem futile.

Well, not futile. *Feudal.*

Feudalism* is a very general name for the system that runs Europe in the Middle Ages. It allows kings to feed and muster armies. It works like this:

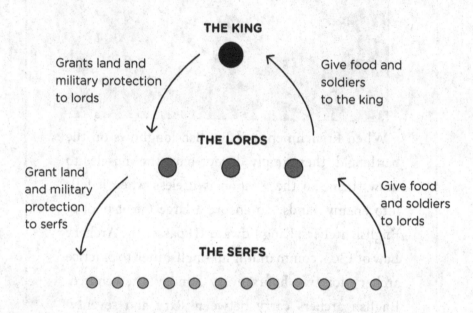

THE KING

Grants land and military protection to lords

Give food and soldiers to the king

THE LORDS

Grant land and military protection to serfs

Give food and soldiers to lords

THE SERFS

Feudalism† is pretty good if you happen to be a lord or a king. If you're a peasant, or "serf," stuck at the bottom of the social ladder, it's less pleasant. A peasant farmer working for a lord lives

---

* Finn Greenquill is a *big* fan of feudalism. However, Time Corp's fact-checking department would like to point out that "feudalism" is a word no longer used by modern scholars. The word does not exist in the Middle Ages, and is too general to describe absolutely everything that's going on across all the countries in Europe over so many centuries.

† As you travel throughout Europe, you will find plenty of exceptions to the chart above. Many kings do not have much power over their lords. And many lords hire professional soldiers for battle, rather than use untrained serfs. Nevertheless, wherever you go, you will find rich lords ruling over lots of poor peasant farmers.

a long, hard life of servitude.* The peasant must farm the lord's land for no pay. The peasant's reward for all this free work is mostly that they are allowed to live on the lord's land, under his protection. If you are given the choice, be a lord. Otherwise, you're better off going to live in a city that isn't run by a lord. Better yet, go live in a different century where all the rules are a bit more fair.

PEOPLE TO HAVE LUNCH WITH:
Jeanne de Clisson

Jeanne de Clisson is a French pirate. She is nicknamed "the Lioness of Brittany." She really deserves her own book, but the Time Corp writing staff is already overworked as it is.

* Or, too often, a *short,* hard life of servitude.

Jeanne is born in 1300. At the ripe old age of twelve, she marries a nineteen-year-old nobleman named Geoffrey. Jeanne has her first son when she's fourteen, and a daughter when she's sixteen. Sadly, her husband dies when Jeanne is twenty-three. So she marries her second husband when she's twenty-eight, but the pope annuls the marriage. Finally, at age thirty, Jeanne marries a nobleman named Olivier and the marriage sticks. She has five more kids.

All is just jim-dandy until Jeanne is forty-three, and French King Philip VI arrests Olivier on suspicion of treason. Even though the king has no proof, he chops off Olivier's head. Olivier's body is hung up on the Paris gallows and his head is displayed on the tip of a spear.

When Jeanne sees her husband's head decorating the city gates, she vows revenge on the French king. She sells all her land and uses the money to build her famous "Black Fleet": a set of pirate ships painted black with blood-red sails. She names her flagship *My Revenge*.

According to legend, for the next thirteen years, Jeanne's pirate army attacks French castles and burns French villages. She captures French ships and per-sonally beheads noblemen with an ax. Every time she murders a crew, she allows one prisoner to escape to spread the word of her terror. In 1346, she helps supply the English troops at the Battle of Crécy. Even when King Philip VI dies, Jeanne continues her war against the French.

In one adventure, Jeanne's ship is sunk and she is forced to escape in a rowboat. For five days, she rows toward England. One of her young sons dies of exposure along the journey, but Jeanne keeps rowing. When she arrives in England, the English are so impressed, they give her a brand-new ship.

Finally, when Jeanne is fifty-six, she marries her fourth husband, a British nobleman named Sir Walter Bentley. He must have a calming effect on her, because Jeanne retires from piracy and lives out the rest of her days in a castle on the French coast.

If you have lunch with Jeanne, make sure she leaves her ax at the door. And for heaven's sake, stay on her good side.

The Battle of Agincourt

This is another amazing battle worth dropping in on. Enter Friday, October 25, 1415, into your time machine and get psyched to fight in one of the most astounding military upsets in history.

The French have quickly learned to hate English archers, and want to send a message. They capture three hundred English bowmen at a town called Soissons. The French torture and mutilate the archers before raping and killing all the town's inhabitants for supporting the English. Point taken.

Henry V, king of England, wants to avenge the English archers. The town of Soissons is dedicated to St. Crispin, and

October 25 is the holiday of St. Crispin's Day. So it is on October 25 that Henry V leads his army to battle against the French. There's just one problem: the French outnumber the English six to one.

STRING YOUR BOW AND
GET READY . . .

Henry V has been marching all over France trying to get the French to fight. But the French army keeps hiding. They are waiting for Henry's army to grow tired and weak. As months pass, Henry's soldiers spend less time fighting, and more time running out of food, getting sick, and dying off. Most of his knights and infantry are soon dearly departed. Henry's army is now almost entirely archers.

Meanwhile, the French army has swelled to enormous size. Nearly every knight in France joins the army, sensing glory and an easy victory over the badly outnumbered English.

THE BATTLEFIELD

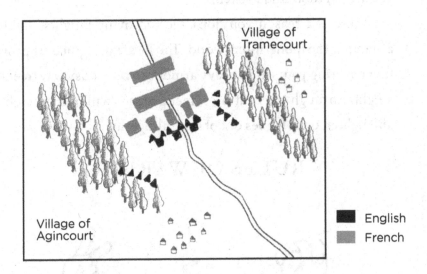

Village of
Tramecourt

Village of
Agincourt

■ English
■ French

THE OUTNUMBERED ENGLISH

The battlefield near the village of Agincourt is covered in mud from recent rains. When the thirty thousand French soldiers march toward Henry's tiny army of archers, they are quickly bogged down in the mud. The French knights are wearing up to sixty pounds of plate armor, and become exhausted after a few minutes of marching. The forests on either side of the battlefield crowd all the French knights together. Soon, many of the French knights are so packed in, they cannot even draw their swords.

The English archers now have a field day, filling the air with their arrows. The French knights are so exhausted from marching through the foot-deep mud, some of them drown when they collapse in their heavy armor and don't have the strength to push themselves back up. The outnumbered English archers slaughter at least ten thousand Frenchmen.

There is a reason you don't see too many knights walking around in the modern-day world. The Battle of Agincourt proves that covering yourself in heavy armor can be a lousy way to enter a fight. Through the centuries, metal armor will become lighter and lighter, until it goes out of style altogether.

RULES OF WARFARE

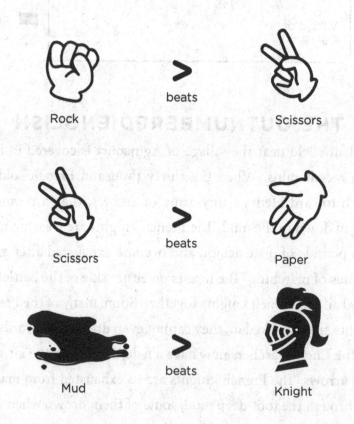

Rock   >   Scissors
       beats

Scissors   >   Paper
          beats

Mud   >   Knight
      beats

PEOPLE TO HAVE LUNCH WITH:
JOAN OF ARC

Joan is a peasant born in a small village in eastern France in 1412. She can neither read nor write, but hardly anybody in the Middle Ages can, so cut her some slack, all right?* Okay, where were we . . . Ah yes. When Joan is thirteen, she begins having visions of saints who tell her to support the French king, Charles VII, and drive the English out of France.

At age sixteen, Joan correctly predicts an English victory at a battle many miles away. This helps convince local French leaders that maybe Joan really can talk to saints and angels. Either that, or they have no

* Due to budget cuts, the Time Corp travel writers did not get their coffee this morning.

better ideas for how to inspire the exhausted French army that is nearing collapse. Joan's saints and angels tell her she can beat the English army out of the town of Orléans, and King Charles VII decides he's willing to try anything at this point. Joan cuts her hair short, dresses like a boy, puts on armor, and leads the remaining French army against the English.

She never carries a sword, only a banner. But it changes the entire battle. Suddenly, the French soldiers believe that God is on their side. If Joan is really chatting with saints and angels, maybe she can put in a good word for them. After five months of stalemate, the tide suddenly turns in favor of the French soldiers. On the morning of May 7, 1429, Joan takes an arrow in the shoulder, but still manages to rally the French to victory.

Joan restores the confidence of the French army. They go on the aggressive, winning a string of victories in 1429. On May 23, 1430, the English ambush and capture Joan in a town called Margny. They put Joan on trial and sentence her to death for wearing armor, dressing like a boy, and claiming to be under God's command. On May 30, 1431, the English burn Joan at the stake. They then collect her ashes and throw them in the Seine River. With Joan gone, the war will rage on for another few decades.

HeLpfuL HiNts:
femaLe fiGHteRs

Were Joan of Arc and Jeanne de Clisson the only women to put on armor and fight in a battle? Not by a long shot. In the Middle Ages, you can hardly walk to the end of your driveway without being attacked by a woman warrior. Meet . . .

SIX DEADLY FEMALE FIGHTERS OF THE MIDDLE AGES

1. **Blanche of Castile, Queen of France,** leads several armies into battle, including a winter surprise attack against a rebellious baron.

2. **Countess Petronilla of Leicester** straps on armor in the English rebellion against Henry II.

3. **Nicola de la Haye,** the sheriff of Lincolnshire, successfully defends Lincoln Castle against an army of four hundred English invaders in 1191.

4. **Empress Matilda** leads military attacks in the English civil war in 1139.

5. **Melisende, Queen of Jerusalem,** commands an army during the Second Crusade.

6. The Order of the Hatchet is not just one woman, but a whole group of female warriors who defeat the Moors attacking the Spanish city of Tortosa. The women free the city in 1149 and are all raised to knighthood.

MEANWHILE, IN WEST AFRICA

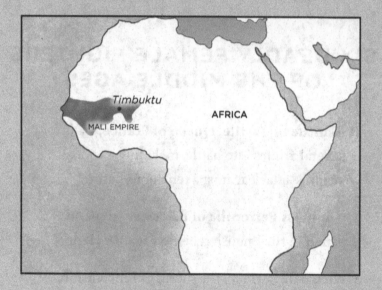

Now might be another good time to take a break in a more peaceful and prosperous part of the world. Why not head down to West Africa and pop in on the empire of Mali?

Mansa Musa is the tenth king of the Mali Empire. He controls half the world's supply of salt and gold.

Many historians consider him the richest person of all time.*

Mansa Musa is a devout Muslim. Time travel to 1324 and you can join Mansa Musa's pilgrimage to visit Mecca in the Middle East.† Mansa Musa travels with a caravan of sixty thousand men, including twelve thousand slaves dressed in Persian silk. For spending money, he brings along eighty camels carrying three hundred pounds of gold each.

In Africa, he ships in architects from Spain and Egypt to help transform his capital of Timbuktu into a world-class city. He expands the University of Sankoré so that it can house twenty-five thousand students as well as one of the largest libraries in Africa, with roughly one million manuscripts. The university still operates today.

CONCLUSION OF THE WAR

The English and French don't fight the longest war in European history without learning a couple of lessons. Now that upper-class knights can be beaten by lower-class bowmen, chivalry

* Finn Greenquill is still hoping to claim this title. He sleeps with a picture of Mansa Musa under his pillow.

† Mecca is a holy city for Muslims because it is the birthplace of the founder of the religion, the prophet Muhammad, and the place where he received his first visions. Muslims try to make a pilgrimage to Mecca at least once in their lives.

begins to wane. Knights are replaced by professional soldiers. England and France form the first permanent armies since the Roman Empire.

For the next few centuries, the English and French never truly stop fighting. They just take breaks once in a while. For instance, anyone who's read that most incredible book *The Thrifty Guide to the American Revolution* knows the French and English will spend a good chunk of the 1700s trying to kill each other.

The Hundred Years' War fizzles out for a variety of reasons. France becomes much better at defending itself, and the English run out of money to fund the war. More importantly, a plague hits Europe that destroys armies far more effectively than any longbow. Between war and plague, France loses half its population by the end of the Hundred Years' War. Paris alone loses two-thirds of its population. Normandy loses a whopping three-quarters of its population. Europe is simply drained of its will to fight.

What was this enormous plague that devastated Europe? Make sure your inoculations are up to date—you're about to find out in the next chapter.

TIME CORP! ™ **SERVING YESTERDAY, FOR A BETTER TOMORROW, TODAY.**™

LETTERS FROM TIME CORP'S COMPLAINT DEPARTMENT

Office of Jillian Mortimer
Assistant to the Second Assistant
of the Vice Assistant's Executive Assistant
Complaint Department

Valued Customer,

A few of you have filed complaints because the Time Corp Complaint Department is no longer responding to complaints. Look, whatever you're complaining about happened way back in the Middle Ages. That was, like, a thousand years ago. Get over it already!

Since a few of you won't stop your whining, I'm going to reply to some complaints here:

Complaint: "I accidentally fought on the French side at the Battle of Agincourt. I called Time Corp for help, but they didn't rescue me in time!"

—Sally S., Newton, MA

Answer: Hey, genius, you're visiting the *Late* Middle Ages, not the *On-Time* Middle Ages.

Complaint: "My hair needed a trim. I visited a medieval barber and asked him to take a little off the sides. He removed both my arms. Please excuse any typos— I am typing this complaint with my nose."

—Hugo P., San Jose, CA

Answer: Hugo, are you sure he didn't remove your brain? Chapter 1 clearly states you should never, ever visit a doctor or barber in the Middle Ages. Please excuse any typos—I am typing this answer with the world's tiniest violin.

Complaint: "I thought angels and saints were talking to me. Turns out I was just being pranked by some time travelers. Now I'm stuck in an English prison. They're going to burn me at the stake in the morning."

—Joan of Arc

Answer: Sorry, Joan, it's my lunch hour. Then I'm taking off early for a weekend in the Poconos. I'll be sure to get right on this sometime in the coming weeks.

Thank you, customers, for your important feedback. Time Corp values your continued loyalty.

Jillian Mortimer
Complaint Department
Time Corp

7

THE BLACK DEATH

THINGS YOU WILL NEED

1. Kleenex
2. Some vitamin C
3. Your affairs in order
4. A will*

The Black Death is a horrific plague that devastates Europe in the mid-1300s.† Somewhere between 75 million and 200 million people are killed worldwide. That's anywhere between 30 and 60 percent of the people on the Eurasian continent. And you thought the Mongols were bad!

....

* Anti-Black Plague pills are available from Time Corp for the reasonable sum of $99,999. Please note: if you don't take our pills, Time Corp is not responsible for your death. Time Corp: our prices are to die for!

† The Black Death was also the name of Finn Greenquill's heavy metal band in high school.

Sensible time travelers may be wondering, why would anyone want to visit a plague? Well, you probably paid for the medieval travel package because of the unbelievably low prices. And now you're learning an important lesson: you get what you pay for.

Remember, at least *one in three* Europeans die from this plague. Think about that! Look to the person on your right. Now look to the person on your left. Do they seem healthy? Then bad news: you are going to die of bubonic plague.

On the upside, at least you got an amazing bargain with Time Corp's low, low prices!

The Beginning of the Plague

Scientists believe the plague starts in central Asia. It kills tens of millions in China alone. The disease spreads westward along trade routes through India, Persia, and the Middle East. In October 1347, a fleet of trading ships lands in Italy. The ships are filled with sick sailors. Their skin is covered in black boils and they're coughing blood. The smart move would be to send them right back to sea, but it's too late and the damage is done. Pretty soon, all of southern Italy is taking a sick day. And then, all of Europe.

Helpful Hints:
the dancing plague of 1518

It's worth a quick visit to Strasbourg* in 1518 to see just how bad plagues are in Europe before modern medicine. Of the many pestilences to ravage the countryside, one of the more bizarre ones is the dancing plague.

It all starts in July 1518, when a Strasbourg woman named Mrs. Troffea begins dancing in the street. She just can't stop the feeling. She dances day and night. By the end of the week, thirty-four people have joined her. By the end of the summer, there are four hundred dancers.

Doctors are called in, but it's 1518, so they're basically medieval doctors, and we all know how that goes. The doctors decide it's best to just let everyone dance the plague out of their system. Town officials hire musicians and build dance halls to house all the dancers. The party continues.

Soon, dancers begin dying of strokes, heart attacks, and exhaustion. The bodies pile up at a rate of fifteen people per day. To this day, science cannot explain this plague. It may be that pop singer Selena Gomez was right all along: sooner or later, the rhythm *does* take you over.

---

* In present-day France.

Treatments for the Black Plague

The nutcases running around Europe calling themselves doctors in 1347 have no idea how to deal with infectious diseases. Let's face it: having no doctor at all is better than having a medieval doctor. They don't know what's causing the plague and they certainly don't know how to stop it.

Some doctors think bad smells can prevent patients from catching the plague, so they make their patients sniff animal dung or urine. Patients are even instructed to store their farts in jars. Then, if they feel a touch of plague coming on, patients unscrew their fart jars and inhale deeply.

A rumor spreads that drinking alcohol safeguards you from the plague. So people begin drinking with abandon. An untold number of Europeans simply drink themselves to death.*

Some particularly brilliant doctors decide that the plague can be caused by taking baths. Bathing, as any medieval doctor can tell you, opens the skin pores, allowing bad spirits to enter the body. The upshot is that soon, many Europeans think it will literally kill them to take a bath.†

....

* So, to be fair, drinking does prevent these people from dying of plague.

† With nobody bathing, it's no coincidence that perfume and cologne become popular in the Late Middle Ages.

Helpful Hints:
The Wolves of Paris

To give you an idea of just how bad life in Europe gets during the Late Middle Ages, sometime around 1437, Paris is invaded by an army of man-eating wolves. The wolves take up residence inside the city during the freezing winter and devour dozens of citizens.

It's rarely fair to blame the victim, but in this case, the Parisians kind of have it coming. By overhunting all the deer and wild boar living around Paris, the Parisians have left the local wolves without any food. The wolf invasion begins with a pack of twenty wolves, led by a reddish wolf that the French name Courtaud. The Paris walls are two hundred years old and in poor repair, so it's easy for Courtaud's band to sneak inside the city.

Courtaud's wolf pack begins dining on women, children, and homeless people. It's such easy pickings that more wolves move to Paris to join the feast. Soon, two or three French people are dying from wolf attacks every single day.

The Parisians decide enough is enough. They slaughter a couple of cows and drag them through the streets with ropes, leaving a bloody trail to attract Courtaud's pack. The trail leads the wolves to the Notre-Dame Cathedral in the center of Paris. There, the Parisians spring a trap, throwing up barricades and pelting the wolves with rocks and spears until they are all killed.

Massacres

The Black Death is now crushing Europe. Everyone wants people to stop dying, so they hit upon a novel solution: kill more people.

Frightened townspeople begin blaming anyone they can for the Black Plague. What can be causing this pestilence? Jewish people practice a different religion and are therefore deemed to be suspicious. Members of the Catholic Church start torturing Jewish people to make them confess to causing the Black Plague.

Catholic priests and church officials rile up their congregations. Panicked townspeople hunt down Jewish people and kill them by the thousands. Remember those jolly dancers in Strasbourg in 1518? Here in 1349, the people of Strasbourg round up two thousand Jewish people and burn them alive at the stake. Similar attacks occur in more than five hundred European towns and cities. Foreigners, beggars, religious pilgrims, friars, Muslims, Romani people* and even lepers are caught and executed as well. To the townspeople's surprise, none of this stops the Black Plague.

The Inquisition

Who are these church members running around imprisoning and killing people? How can you be a Catholic and work in a torture chamber at the same time? Welcome to one of the least pleasant parts of the Middle Ages: the Inquisition.

The Inquisition is a sort of police force working for the Catholic Church. Their job is to find and punish anyone who doesn't follow the exact rules of Catholicism. If you meet any of these Inquisitors in your travels, keep your distance. They are allowed to torture you until you confess to a crime. Luckily for them, it turns out people will confess to just about anything if they are tortured long enough.

....

* The Romani people are a semi-nomadic group originally from northwestern India, who first settle in Europe in the Early Middle Ages.

If you confess to not holding the proper religious beliefs, the Inquisitors can burn you at the stake, crush you under a pile of rocks, or drown you. According to their rules, they can do pretty much anything they like to you as long as it doesn't draw blood (hence the love for burning, crushing, drowning, and other creative ways of making life unpleasant).

Ghettos

Across Europe, Jewish people are moved into ghettos. These are walled-off sections of cities that Jewish people are only allowed out of during the day.

In 1492, the Spanish government is badly in debt from years of war.* Spain decides to steal all of the wealth from its Jewish population and kick them out of the country. They kick the Muslims out as well. Spain uses stolen Jewish money to fund a man named Christopher Columbus, who needs ships to try to discover a faster trade route to Asia.

....
* It took many years of fighting, but in 1492, the Spanish Christians finally defeat the last remaining Muslims in Spain.

Helpful Hints:
the Law

If you are accused of a crime, it's important to know your rights. Before you can be subjected to thumbscrews or stretched on a torture rack, you are given the right to a fair trial. During a large part of the Middle Ages, a fair trial may happen in several ways:

1. Ordeal by Fire: You must hold a red-hot iron bar and walk three paces. If your hand heals after three days, good news! You're innocent. Plus, your hand is healed! If not, you are guilty, and your scarred hand is the least of your worries. Enjoy the thumbscrews.

2. Ordeal by Water: Same thing as the Ordeal by Fire, except you have to stick your hand in boiling water. If your hand heals in three days—great! You're innocent! If you don't heal, say hello to the thumbscrews.

3. Ordeal by Combat: If you are a nobleman, you may choose trial by combat. You challenge your accuser to a fight to the death. Whoever wins is right. Whoever loses is dead and therefore clearly guilty.

If you think any of this sounds at all unreasonable, consider that it is normal to sue animals in court in the Middle Ages. In one case, mice are publicly tried for stealing grain. In another court case, a swarm of locusts is convicted for eating crops.

WHAT TO DO IF YOU ARE IMPRISONED FOR WITCHCRAFT

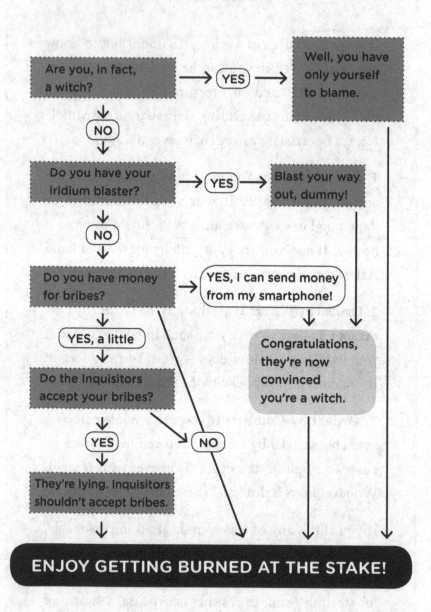

Are you, in fact, a witch? → YES → Well, you have only yourself to blame.

NO

Do you have your iridium blaster? → YES → Blast your way out, dummy!

NO

Do you have money for bribes? → YES, I can send money from my smartphone!

YES, a little

Do the Inquisitors accept your bribes? → NO

YES

They're lying. Inquisitors shouldn't accept bribes.

Congratulations, they're now convinced you're a witch.

ENJOY GETTING BURNED AT THE STAKE!

Christopher Columbus

Christopher Columbus starts out life working at his father's cheese stand. He grows up to become an accomplished sailor, and he has a big idea. Like many people in the Middle Ages, Columbus knows the earth is round, and he thinks that by sailing across the Atlantic Ocean, he can find a faster trade route to Asia.

HOW COLUMBUS THINKS THE WORLD IS

HOW THE WORLD ACTUALLY IS

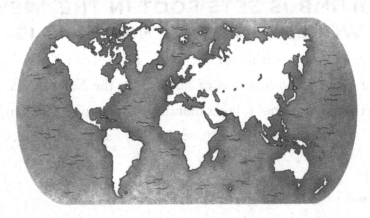

The current trade routes to Asia have a lot of middlemen.* If you live in Italy and want to buy some silk from China, the price has probably been marked up by every trader from Bukhara to Baghdad. To top it off, when the Ottoman Turks capture Constantinople in 1453, prices for Asian goods skyrocket. Europe desperately needs a better way to trade with Asia.

The Italian government thinks Columbus's plan of sailing west across the Atlantic to reach Asia is ridiculous. They refuse to give him any money for ships. When Columbus asks the Portuguese for help, they laugh him out of their country.

It is the Spanish government that decides to roll the dice. They soon sign a contract with Columbus. If his crazy trip succeeds, he will be named "Admiral of the Ocean Sea," but that's not all. Columbus will also become governor over all the land he can claim for Spain. But wait, there's more! Columbus and his descendants will be granted 10 percent of all the money generated by the new lands ... *for all time!*

COLUMBUS SETS FOOT IN THE "NEW WORLD"—NEW TO *HIM*, THAT IS

Set your time machine for August 3, 1492, when Columbus's crew leaves Spain in a fleet of three ships: the *Niña*, the *Pinta*, and the *Santa María*. It takes months to sail across the Atlantic. At two in the morning on October 12, they finally sight land. Co-

---

* After all, this is the Middle Ages.

lumbus believes he has discovered a new route to Asia. But he has actually stumbled upon two entire continents unknown to the Europeans: the Americas.

The Santa Maria

Décor: ★
Wi-Fi: No ✕
Service: ★
Restrooms: None ✕
Cost: $
Ambiance: Casual
Attire: No shoes
Outdoor Seating: Yes

Time travelers who think it's a fun idea to sail with Columbus to discover America usually haven't read the fine print. Columbus's lead ship, the *Santa María*, is tiny—only one hundred feet long—barely larger than Finn Greenquill's moon golf cart. There are no bunks belowdecks, so fifty-two men must find places to sleep on the main deck.* There are no bathrooms; if you need to go, the ocean is your toilet.

Most of the sailors cannot read or write. Four are criminals who chose working on a ship as an alternative to prison time. Most of the sailors go barefoot to avoid slipping on the wet deck. Food is served out of a communal pot. There are no utensils, so each sailor uses his work knife to stab at his food.

....

* Once hammocks are discovered in the New World, Europeans quickly begin using hammocks for beds belowdecks.

The only food on board is bread, biscuits, salted beef, anchovies, and sardines. You're basically going to eat the same meal every day for three months. To drink, you can have wine or stale water. Food is rationed because no one knows how long the voyage will take. Anyone who steals more than their daily food ration is whipped.

Life on board is hard. Raising, lowering, and mending sails. Steering the ship, swabbing the deck. But don't worry—for your troubles you'll be paid one thousand Spanish *maravedís* per month.*

Here is what some of our readers say about the *Santa María:*

★★ "I was looking forward to the sardines, but I was too seasick to eat."   —Shin L., Oklahoma City, OK

★ "If I have to eat one more anchovy, I'm going to mutiny."
                                        —Mark N., Houston, TX

★★★★ "Everyone on the ship had a wonderful time and loved the food."   —Christopher C., Genoa, Italy

Columbus: Good Explorer, Bad Governor

Columbus creates the first Spanish settlements in the New World. The Americas become a huge source of wealth for Spain, introducing new crops for Europe, as well as a vast new source of gold and silver. Columbus is cruel and violent to the Native Americans who already inhabit his "New World."

---

* About $6.95.

When the Spanish government finds out how badly Columbus is treating the Native Americans, they throw him in prison. The Spanish rulers never give Columbus 10 percent of the money made from the Americas; they keep it all for themselves.

HeLpfuL HiNts:
top five iNveNtioNs of tHe miᵭᵭLe ages

Time Corp's legal department has made sure this travel guide is extremely clear on how horrifically dangerous the Middle Ages are. But this does not do complete justice to the time period. Many nifty gadgets we now take for granted are invented in medieval times: wheelbarrows, horseshoes, heavy plows, mechanical clocks, oil paint, mirrors, and even mousetraps. Here are the top five inventions of the Middle Ages.*

1. Eyeglasses: An Italian named Alessandro di Spina is credited with introducing the first eyeglasses to Europe around 1280. The glasses do not sit on the face, but are held by a handle. In the 1600s, Spaniards will add silk ribbons that can tie the spectacles to your ears. It is not until 1727 that a British eye doctor

* According to Finn Greenquill's personal opinions.

named Edward Scarlett invents glasses with arms that hook around your ears while resting on your nose.

2. Universities: Universities first appear elsewhere in the world, from India to Morocco. In the Middle Ages, Europe starts catching up, founding impressive universities, many of which still exist today. The University of Bologna, for example, is founded in Italy in 1088 and is still going strong.

3. Poetry: Okay, okay, fine. Poetry was invented way before the Middle Ages. But have you read Dante Alighieri from Italy? Have you read Geoffrey Chaucer from England? Have you read Marie de France from, well, France? These poets transform the art and help define their national languages. To this day, Dante is considered the most important writer in Italian history.

4. Parliament: England's parliament starts in 1258. At the time, all of Europe is ruled by kings. But England takes some of the first steps toward democracy by stating that the English king must get the approval of the nation's lords before raising new taxes.

5. Banks: Finn Greenquill chose this list, and Finn Greenquill loves banks. Banks let you borrow money. Banks also let you deposit money in one branch, and withdraw it from another. The ideas behind modern banks develop in the High Middle Ages. The Knights Templar, whom you remember from page 67, became astonishingly wealthy from these innovations.

Every Black Plague Has a Silver Lining

If you are reading this sentence good news—you are still alive! Against all odds, you have survived the Middle Ages!

Times are changing in Europe. Miraculously, the Black Plague improves society in unexpected ways. With so many people dead, many farms cannot continue to run. As a result, peasants leave their farms, leave their lords, and move into towns and cities to learn trades. The few remaining farmers are now in high demand, so many of them can demand lower rents and lift themselves out of poverty.

In the 1440s, a German named Johannes Gutenberg invents the first printing press. Instead of being hand-copied in monasteries, books can now be printed quickly and cheaply. More people can suddenly afford books and have a reason to learn to read. This new crop of European bookworms rediscover the work of the great thinkers of ancient Greece and Rome.

New exploration and trade routes lead to a greater exchange of ideas between cultures. Increasing trade creates new wealth that is spent encouraging the arts. By the 1470s, a new generation of artistic geniuses is born. Names like Michelangelo, Botticelli, and Leonardo da Vinci will ring throughout history as they paint and sculpt world-class masterpieces.

For a thousand years, Europe has been mired in illiteracy, poverty, famine, and war. Now, there is a rebirth of knowledge, called the Renaissance.*

But the Renaissance is a story for another Thrifty time travel adventure. . . .

....
* *Renaissance* is a very old French word for "rebirth."

TIME CORP!™ SERVING YESTERDAY, FOR A BETTER TOMORROW, TODAY.™

MIDDLE AGES EXIT SURVEY
TIME CORP SURVEY DEPARTMENT

Wow! After meeting Huns, Vikings, Mongols, and plagues, you actually survived your trip to the Middle Ages! It would not be going out on a limb to say you probably lost a few limbs. If you still have both your hands, give yourself a high five! If you only have one hand, that is all you will need to complete this survey.

1. Please rank your experiences in the Middle Ages:

	Not Satisfactory	Satisfactory	Very Satisfactory
Being hunted by Huns	○	○	○
Being mangled by Mongols	○	○	○
Being burned at the stake	○	○	○
Catching the Black Plague	○	○	○

2. Do you have any money left? If yes, which extremely safe Thrifty time travel package would you like to spend even more money on next?
A. *The Thrifty Guide to the Dinosaur Extinction*
B. *The Thrifty Guide to the San Francisco Earthquake*

C. *The Thrifty Guide to the Eruption of Mount Vesuvius*

D. *The Thrifty Guide to the Tsunami of 1755*

3. Do you have suggestions for how Time Corp can improve our quality service? If you do, on a scale of 1–5, how much do you think we care?

(please circle one)   1   2   3   4   5

4. On a scale of 1–5, how much do you like the number 6?

(please circle one)   1   2   3   4   5

5. On a scale of 9–10, how great is Finn Greenquill?

(please circle one)   9   10

Your answers are important to us! We hope your trip to the Middle Ages was very satisfactory, or satisfactory, or not satisfactory.

Sincerely,

The Time Corp Survey Department

Please note: if you have any complaints for the Time Corp Survey Department, you may contact Jillian Mortimer in the Complaint Department at:

A. Time Corp Headquarters

B. Her home

C. Her cell phone

Ⓓ None of the above

SELECTED BIBLIOGRAPHY

Asbridge, Thomas. *The Crusades: The Authoritative History of the War for the Holy Land*. New York: Ecco, 2011.

Brownworth, Lars. *The Sea Wolves: A History of the Vikings*. United Kingdom: Crux Publishing Ltd, 2014.

Gies, Frances, and Joseph Gies. *Life in a Medieval Village*. New York: Harper Perennial, 1991.

Kahn, Paul, based on the translation by Francis Woodman Cleaves. *The Secret History of the Mongols*. Boston: Cheng & Tsui Company, 1998.

Newman, Paul B. *Daily Life in the Middle Ages*. Jefferson, North Carolina: McFarland & Company, Incorporated Publishers, 2001.

Polo, Marco. *The Travels of Marco Polo*. New York: Penguin Classics, 1958.

Seward, Desmond. *The Hundred Years War: The English in France 1337–1453*. New York: Penguin Books, 1999.

ACKNOWLEDGMENTS

The travel writers at Time Corp would like to thank bug spray, bear spray, and nasal spray for helping us survive our research trips to the Middle Ages.

A special thanks to Leila Sales, who is a much better editor than Finn Greenquill, and an all-around better person, too. A very appreciative thank-you to editor Sheila Keenan for stepping in and pinch-hitting! A big thank-you to the copyeditors Laura Stiers and Janet Pascal for bringing the Age of Reason to the Dark Ages of my spelling and grammar. A tip of the hat to expert reader Sam Sutherland, whose depth of knowledge makes the Mariana Trench look like a puddle. And a hearty thank-you to art director Jim Hoover and junior designer Mariam Quraishi for classing up the charts and layout; Johannes Gutenberg would be very proud indeed.

No wolves, bears, or Mongols were harmed in the writing of this book.

Jonathan W. Stokes is a former teacher turned Hollywood screenwriter, who has written screenplays for Warner Brothers, Universal, Fox, Paramount, New Line, and Sony/Columbia. Inspired by a childhood love of *The Goonies* and *Ferris Bueller's Day Off*, Jonathan writes the Addison Cooke series as well as the other books in the Thrifty Guide series. Raised in Connecticut, he currently resides in Los Angeles, where he can be found showing off his incredible taste in dishware and impressive 96 percent accuracy with high fives.

Follow him on Twitter @JonathanWStokes or Instagram @inStokesgram.

Xavier Bonet is an illustrator and a comic book artist who lives in Barcelona with his wife and two children. He has illustrated a number of middle grade books, including *Omnia* by Laura Gallego, Michael Dahl's Really Scary Stories series, and the Keepers trilogy by Lian Tanner. He loves all things retro, video games, and Japanese food, but above all, spending time with his family.

Visit him at xavierbonet.net and follow him on Twitter or Instagram @xbonetp.

KEEP TRAVELING THROUGH TIME!

Wherever you go on your next vacation,
be sure to bring along a Thrifty Guide to get
the most out of your blast to the past!

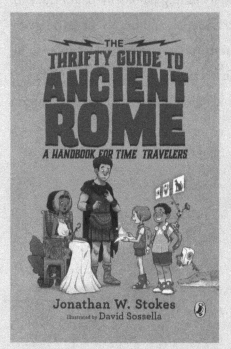

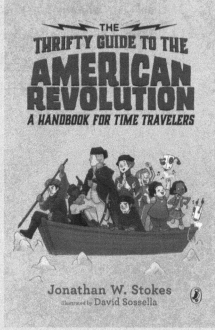

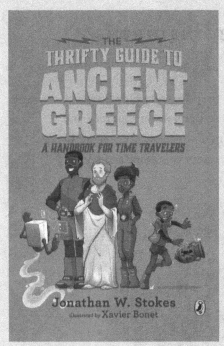

WANT TO SEE MORE?

Turn the page for sneak peeks at the greatest travel guides in all history—and we know because we checked all of history!

Thrifty Guides: Don't leave the 21st century without one!

TOP FIVE WAYS TO DIE IN ROME

1. Fire

If you are a pyromaniac, Rome is the place to be. Fires break out so frequently, you can grab a snack, climb up on your roof, and watch the town burn. Homes burn down nearly every night, an entire neighborhood burns down every two years, and the en-

tire city burns down completely in AD 64. This is because open fires and olive oil lamps are the only source of fuel and light. In its early days, for bonus flammability, many of Rome's buildings are wooden structures with thatched straw roofs, built incredibly close together. If you are trying to build a combustible city, you can't do better than Rome with this winning combination of open flames and a complete lack of fire codes. If you're visiting Rome, bring marshmallows.

2. Flood

Time Corp's legal department requires us to mention that if the fires don't kill you, the floods probably will. The Tiber River provides Rome with transportation and trade, but regularly drowns Romans by flooding its banks a few times a year. In severe floods, the Tiber may surge 30 feet above its normal level, carrying

entire apartment buildings downstream. When your apartment collapses, you're going to have a bad time. Perhaps most disturbingly, Rome's sewage system is tied to the water level. So every time there's a flood, many of Rome's toilets back up and empty into the streets. Don't say we didn't warn you.

WHEN IN ROME...

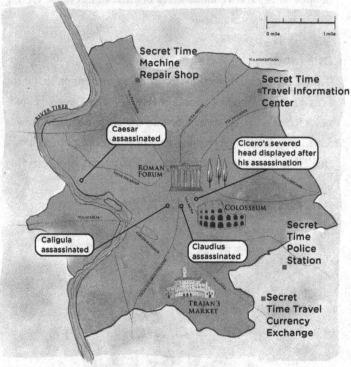

MAP OF PLACES WHERE PEOPLE GET KILLED (A.K.A. ROME)

Secret Time Machine Repair Shop

Secret Time Travel Information Center

Caesar assassinated

Cicero's severed head displayed after his assassination

ROMAN FORUM

COLOSSEUM

Caligula assassinated

Claudius assassinated

Secret Time Police Station

TRAJAN'S MARKET

Secret Time Travel Currency Exchange

RIVER TIBER

0 mile   1 mile

Getting Around in Ancient Rome

Sure, the Greeks came up with the grid system, but the Romans took city planning to a whole new level. Nearly all Romans live in apartment buildings called *insulae*. These concrete apartment buildings are up to ten stories high and can take up entire city blocks. There are fifty thousand apartment buildings in Rome. They're fairly modern in many ways, except they have the unfortunate habit of collapsing.

By the empire's peak, Rome's 113 provinces are connected by 372 paved highways. That's more than 50,000 miles of paved roads, many of which survive for thousands of years. France alone contains 13,000 miles of Roman roadways.

If you're trying to blend into Roman society, hoverboards are surprisingly conspicuous. The best way to see the sights without upsetting the locals is on a horse.

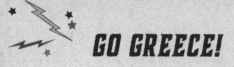

Athenian men have the right to vote. Women, slaves, and foreigners do not. One of the things Athenian men can vote for is to ban unpopular people from the city. If six thousand people vote to *ostracize** a citizen, that person must leave Athens for ten years. This, apparently, is how people entertained themselves before reality TV.

THE COURTS

Stopping by the courthouse may not be your idea of fun sightseeing, but keep in mind Athens has the first true courthouses in the world. Centuries earlier, the Athenians elected a man named Draco to create the first written laws in history. It turned out his laws were pretty harsh—according to the Greek philosopher Aristotle, Draco wrote the laws using human blood. Laziness was against the law, and even stealing a cabbage was punishable by death. So the Athenians voted to ostracize Draco. The new Greek laws aren't nearly so harsh, but you still shouldn't steal any cabbages.

FASHION TIPS FOR ANCIENT ATHENS

The key for any time travel disguise is to blend in and look good doing it. Greece is a warm climate, so staying cool is almost as important as looking cool. Follow Time Corp's style guide and no one will suspect you are from the future; they will only suspect you are extremely suave.

* For more on ostracism, see the sidebar on page 65.

MEN'S FASHION

Andreas is wearing this light-weight men's linen chiton tunic from our spring collection, and topping it off with a carefree wool chlamys cloak. These muted colors are perfect for blending in with the common people of Athens, who cannot afford expensive clothing dyes, but cannot afford to not look fabulous. Watch out, Athens! On the street, Andreas wears sensible sandals well-suited for the warm Mediterranean climate. In the home, like many Greeks, Andreas goes barefoot. And why not? Athens is a beach city with a laid-back vibe, and you only live once, people.

WOMEN'S FASHION

Sofia will be hitting this year's food markets in style with this ankle-length, sleeveless peplos tunic that says "because I deserve it." Hold on to your chariots! When she goes out, Sofia will accessorize with a veil and a lavender-dyed himation wrap that

will be turning heads from the assembly all the way to the agora. Like all fashion-conscious Greek women, Sofia wears her tunic much longer than Andreas; Greek men like to show a bit more leg. Sofia is topping off her outfit today with a fierce combination of gold earrings, silver bracelets, and a seashell necklace.

HAIR DOS AND DON'TS IN ANCIENT ATHENS

One of the biggest problems of time travel—besides all the time paradoxes—is that your hairstyle can be thousands of years out of date. You can try telling the Greeks that your haircut is simply 2,600 years ahead of its time, but Finn Greenquill has tried this in many time periods, and it rarely works. Remember, there's never a second chance to make a first impression.[*]

Here are a few quick and handy hair tips . . .

....
[*] Unless you are a time traveler, in which case there are infinite second chances to make a first impression. But still, you get our point—get a decent haircut.

Men

In 480 BC Greek men tend to wear their hair short and grow large beards. If you visit later in Greek history, the beards go out of style. Stay alert, folks. Fashion is like a shark: if it doesn't keep swimming forward, it dies.

Women

Greek women often grow their hair long, braid it, and put it up. Only slave women rock short hair. Later in Greek history, women will favor tying their hair back or wearing it in a bun. Many Greek women bleach their hair by dipping it in vinegar.

Makeup is popular in ancient Greece. Because rich women can afford to stay indoors all day, pale skin equals high status. So Greek women make their skin lighter by covering it in chalk. Wealthier women use white lead because it lasts longer than

REVOLUTION!

January 9, his crew refuses to keep going. They quit and go home to New York. Henry has to hire new men and fresh oxen. It is on January 27, 1776, that Henry Knox finally delivers the cannons to General Washington in Cambridge. The total job took ten weeks and cost 521 pounds.* But Henry does not lose a single cannon on the three-hundred-mile journey.

PRANKING THE PAST

Just when Henry Knox rolls his last cannon into Cambridge . . . transport them all back to Fort Ticonderoga.

HELPFUL HINTS:

WHAT TO EXPECT WHEN YOU'RE EXPECTING . . . TO BE SHOT BY A CANNON

1. If you're on a battlefield and you hear a deafening boom, you may be being shot at by a cannon.

2. If you hear a loud whistling sound, that is the cannonball flying straight toward you.

* This is actually an amazing bargain, considering how much it costs to manufacture British cannons.

Excerpt from *The Thrifty Guide to the American Revolution*
Text copyright © 2018 by Tracy Street Productions, Inc.
Illustrations copyright © 2018 by David Sossella

3. Do not try to outrun the cannonball; it travels eight hundred feet per second, and you don't.

4. Remain calm. There is nothing to be afraid of, aside from death.

5. Shout and wave your arms to make yourself appear larger, to intimidate the cannonball. Oh wait, no. That's if you're attacked by a mountain lion.

6. Quietly back away slowly. Oh wait, sorry. That's if you're charged by a bear.

7. Okay, hang on. Let us think for a second.

8. All right, there's really nothing you can do. Maybe start to panic.

9. Do you have an iridium blaster? Well, that won't help. No one can hit a target moving at eight hundred feet per second.

10. Is this a good time to remind you to purchase Time Corp's very affordable life insurance package for only $999,999,999*?

11. If you feel a slight twinge in your side, like your body is being torn in half, you may be being hit by a cannonball.

12. You probably should have chosen a different vacation package. Thank you for time traveling with Time Corp, where every good decision is made in hindsight.

* With mail-in rebate.

Cannons Are Awesome

A large cannon will fire a cannonball nearly a mile. If the cannonball doesn't kill you on impact, it can kill you on the bounce. A cannonball bouncing through ranks of soldiers in an infantry square can kill dozens. If a cannonball is fired directly into a column of advancing soldiers, it can pass straight through up to forty men. Washington finally has the cannons he needs. This is huge. It's time to put them to work against the British.

Sneaking the Cannons into Position

Set your Time Corp Time Machine Colonial™ for March 4, 1776. Under the cloak of night, you can help General Washington's Continental Army sneak Henry Knox's cannons onto Dorchester Heights. Two thousand patriot workers and 360 oxcarts lug equipment up the hill. Hay bales are placed between the troops

HENRY KNOX'S CANNONS
FIND A NEW HOME

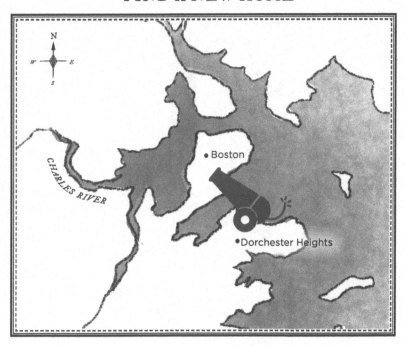

and the harbor in order to stifle the sounds of the moving cannons. Wagon wheels are muffled with straw. General Washington gallops up and down the lines, whispering encouragement to the soldiers. Miraculously, by four in the morning, all the cannon batteries are complete. The Americans can now rain leaden terror down into Boston.